The Romantic Boy
Short Erotical Story Book

Romance Lovers Anywhere

Fiona Rose

About for This Book

🔲 *Explore Passion and Intrigue:* This short story collection blends erotic themes with profound romantic encounters, perfect for igniting your fantasies.

🔲 *Every Story a New Adventure:* Each tale transports you to a world where love, desire, and passion meet, crafted to tantalize the senses and stir the soul.

🔲 *Diverse Settings and Characters:* From spontaneous rendezvous in exotic locales to tender moments in everyday settings, experience a variety of scenarios and characters, all bound by the common thread of romance.

🔲 *For Romance Lovers:* Whether you're a hopeless romantic or a seeker of passionate escapades, these stories cater to all who cherish love's boundless dimensions.

🔲 *Perfect for Quick Reads:* Ideal for those moments when you need a quick escape into a world of romance and eroticism. Each story is short, making fitting into a busy day easy.

Ideal For:

Avid readers of romance and erotic fiction looking for new adventures. Individuals are seeking a quick yet immersive reading experience. Gifts for special occasions to anyone who loves a good love story.

Embark on a passion and intimate exploration journey with Fiona Rose's "The Romantic Boy: Short Erotic Story Book." Your next escape into the world of romance and desire awaits.

Introduction

Are you ready to embark on a journey where passion and romance merge into a compelling blend of desire and love? Welcome to "Romantic Boy Short Erotical Story Book" by Fiona Rose, a collection that promises to captivate the hearts of romance lovers everywhere. Whether you prefer Kindle or paperback, this book is crafted for you, offering an intimate escape into the world of love's deepest emotions.

This collection of stories invites you to lose yourself in the intoxicating embrace of romance. Each tale is designed to draw you in, with vivid characters and gripping plots that will keep you turning pages late into the night. Feel the intensity of first love, the thrill of secret encounters, and the sweetness of enduring affection, all woven into short, compelling narratives.

Imagine curling up with a book that promises to transport you to a place where every heartbeat is a testament to love's power. Fiona Rose's masterful storytelling ensures that each story is not just read but experienced, leaving you longing for more.

Take advantage of this extraordinary collection. Indulge in the allure of romantic escapades, and let these stories ignite your imagination and touch your soul. Purchase "The Romantic Boy Short Erotical Story Book" today and immerse yourself in the best of erotic romance.

Copyright © 2024 by Fiona Rose

All rights reserved.

No part of this book may be reproduced, distributed, or transmitted in any form or by any means, including photocopying, recording, or other electronic or mechanical methods, without the prior written permission of the author, except in the case of brief quotations embodied in critical reviews and specific other non-commercial uses permitted by copyright law, for permission requests.

This is a work of fiction. Names, characters, place, and incidents are either the product of the author's imagination or used fictitiously. Any resemblance to actual persons, living or dead, events, or locales is entirely coincidental.

The author acknowledges the trademarked status and trademark owners of various products referenced in this work of fiction, which have been used without permission. The publication/use of these trademarks is not authorized, associated with, or sponsored by the trademark owners.

This book is licensed for your enjoyment only. It may not be resold or given away to other people. If you would like to share this book with another person, please purchase an additional copy for each recipient. Thank you for respecting the hard work of this author.

Table Of Content

1. Fantasy with Aunty — 01
2. A Gentle Caress to a Cousin — 07
3. Bringing Aunt's Daughter to Bed — 15
4. Which I Gave The Teacher Felt Extreme Happiness — 21
5. Passionate Love for Maid Abandoned by Husband — 36
6. Love with Tenant Aunty — 43
7. The First Happiness of The New Year — 53
8. Mother Fucks Uncle — 64
9. My Child in The Maid's Woman — 69
10. Arpa's Sexual Desire — 86
11. My Baby in The Womb of My Brother's Wife — 98
12. Alienation and Physical Needs of Housewife's — 103
13. My Baby in The Belly of Elder Brother's Wife — 115
14. Mona's Taste of Motherhood — 122

Fantasy with Aunty

Hello, my name is Alin. Today, I am going to tell you another interesting story. This story happened when I was 21 years old. Before that, let me introduce myself. I live in Kolkata city. I just finished college.

Now, let's come to the main story. The incident happened with a cousin of our flat. He will be 42 years old. My name is Maya. We used to call Maya aunty. Give the details of his body. His figure size will be 36-38-40.

The most exciting thing is her breasts. Which will make anyone's penis hard? When he walks down the street, all the men stand up. It has even been heard that many men in our village have relations with him.

I have a weakness for older women, so it was no different in his case. I wanted to fuck him for a long time. But somehow, I could not get up.

One day, when I was exercising, he came to dry clothes on the roof, seeing him made my penis erect. Ahh, what's the matter with my ass? It seems that I hug from behind and start fucking from behind.

My eyes were on the cuckoo's place, how beautiful the breasts were. Now, different stories started between us. Aunty asked me everything about my house. But suddenly,

Aunty asked a strange question: You don't have a girlfriend?

Me – no, Aunty, not yet. Aunty - why do you have to do it?

Me – No, go, I wouldn't say I like it. Aunty - so you want to see my ass and breasts? The sky fell on my head.

Aunty - How many times do you take juice out of your penis when you see me?

I - No, what are you talking about?

Aunty - Ken looked at me on the roof that day. And I noticed that your small penis also looked hard, and the condition was terrible. Aunty - I saw that your penis got hard after seeing me. And to be honest, I haven't had anyone's genitals enter my genitals for a long time. Your cock's 4-inch penis can't calm me down. So I want a young boy's penis like yours. My whole body was electrified. What am I listening to?

I calmed myself down somehow, and when I got home, I went to the bathroom and shook my hand, and calmed my penis down. After that, my attraction to him increased. I used to look for opportunities to fuck Aunty in any way. One day, all my family members went to a relative's house for a wedding.

I did not go to that marriage house on the excuse of ill health. Because I intended to fuck aunty. Morning turned into afternoon. While I was sleeping, there was a knock on the door.

Annoyed, I opened the door and saw Aunty. I was surprised. Maya Aunty came herself. Aunty was wearing a pink saree. Her breasts were visible. My penis got hard.

Aunty - Alin, are you free? Can you help me?
I agreed on one leg. I said - yes, Aunty, tell me what to do?

Aunty - don't watch the TV in our house. Not working, I went and saw that there was no problem with Auntie's TV; the problem was solved very quickly.

Aunty, you are the boss.

Let me bring you some tea,
Aunty said and went to make tea. I sat on the chair. After a while, Aunty brought tea and sat in front of me.

Aunty took my hand and took me to the bedroom. I kissed Aunty's lips for about 20 minutes. Then we parted. I took off Aunty's clothes one by one. First saree, then blouse bra all. Aunty covered her face and was making loud noises. I kissed Aunty again. Then I put her on the bed and started sucking her pussy. Ahhhh, what, honey? A light sweet smell from his pussy. He gently held my hair. And with mouth - ah, um, uf started making such sounds. After about 20 min of pussy sucking, he released the water. Then he said - now it's my turn. I took off my pants.

Aunty – No, it can't be done like this. Stand up. After a while, the aunt brought a bottle of honey and put some on my penis. And then he started licking with his tongue. I had reached the seventh ocean of happiness. Um, by mouth, oh, aunty. Such sounds were coming out. I understand that after that, the semen will come out again. So I told Aunty to stop sucking and lie down. Aunty slept.

I took my thick penis and inserted it straight into her pussy, and he screamed, ahh, I'm dead.

I understand that I have to come and fuck.

So I took out the genitals again and slowly inserted half and the whole genitals. And then I started fucking.

Aunty – Uf, ah, honey, ah fuck me, kill me fuck, ah uf. I fucked Aunty in a missionary position for about 20 minutes. Then I put some oil on Aunty's ass and Fucker her ass for about 15 min. The whole room is just the sound of us fucking and the sound of Aunty screaming. After fucking a 42-year-old woman for about 40 minutes, it was time for me to cum.

I wanted to fuck aunty. I - Aunty will put semen inside the mouth. Aunty started sucking my genitals. Then I poured my entire cum in Aunty's mouth.

In this way, we took some rest after having sex, and then I got dressed and came back home. So Aunty had the opportunity to fuck for the first time. Since then, whenever I got time, I used to go to fuck Aunty, and she felt very peaceful. Thus, I developed a sexual relationship with Aunty. But I didn't cum in his pussy. But I have fucked in the ass many times and have cum there.

When my uncle was not home or went to the office, we hung out when we had time. We even spent the night in the hotel room. I also went to the cinema, shopping, etc. with Aunty.

I sat in a corner of the park and pressed my breasts. But only his sister came to know about our relationship. So she also forced Aunty to fuck me. As a result,

I also fucked his sister several times, and Aunty and her sister were lucky enough to fuck in one bed. I will tell that story another day. So, if this is not the case, I will tell you in any other book.

A Gentle Caress to a Cousin

My name is Jonny. Today, I will tell you about an incident when I was 18. I have just passed the higher secondary examination.

After the exam, I visited my aunt's house for a few days. Aunty, Uncles, and my cousin Eva Morison used to live in the aunt's house. Eva Morison was a few days younger than me. So we were more like friends than brothers and sisters.

Eva Morison looked very beautiful. Although the height is not too high, the figure is excellent. Big and tight breasts. Medium size narrow waist and big round ass. The color of the body is bright brown. There is a sexy expression in the eyes. However, I have always had a soft spot for Eva Morison, but I have never expressed it in any way.
Sometimes seeing her in short dresses or tight dresses would make my Penis hard. But until then.

I never thought that anything more could happen. Anyway, on the third day after going to my aunt's house, my aunt suddenly had diarrhea. As a result, he had to be admitted to the hospital. My aunt and Uncle started waking up in the hospital at night.

Meanwhile, Eva Morison and I are alone at home. Uncle told us to be careful and went to the hospital. After eating at night, after talking for a while, I said, I'm going to sleep; I'm very sleepy. When my aunt came home, I used to sleep in the same room with my Uncle. Aunt and Eva Morison used to sleep in the other room. We have to sleep alone in separate rooms as Aunty is not home.

Eva Morison said, "Listen, neither can I sleep alone; I am terrified, so let's sleep in the same room. 'I said, 'Okay, I don't have any problem.'

Even though I said this in my mouth, thinking about sleeping in the same room with Eva Morison made my heart skip. But I did not express it in my mouth. We took a bath and went to sleep in Uncle's room.

I went to sleep wearing half-pants and a T-shirt, which were silk nighties. While sleeping, Eva Morison put a side pillow between us and said, "See that you don't fall on me again at night." He smiled. I smelled some indulgence in his words. I tried to guess what Oki Fuked. Anyway, I turned off the light and went to bed. But Eva Morison's last words were on my mind. I couldn't sleep at all. On the other hand,

I could hear Eva Morison's exhalation while she was asleep. He seemed to be sleeping. I sat up slowly. Even though the light was off, I could see everything inside the room now in the dim light coming from outside. I noticed that Eva Morison's nightie had gone up above her knees. The runs of his legs are visible. My Penis slowly hardened.

I took off my pants and got naked. Then, I removed the side pillow and moved to Eva Morison. He was sleeping with his butt towards me. I very slowly lifted her nightie further up. Underneath is a panty. Her ass was so beautiful that my Penis became hard as iron.

I slowly tried to pull down her panty. But because he was lying down, even if one side came down, the other did not. I was breathing heavily with excitement. Without thinking, I pulled a little and went to open his pants. And therein lies the danger. Eva Morison woke up and immediately switched on the light.

It all happened so fast that I looked like an idiot. On turning on the light, he saw that I was long and my Penis was erect and straight up. He angrily told me, Shame: This is what you had in mind?

Finally, going to fuck his sister? I cried and said, please don't tell anyone; I made a big mistake and will never repeat it. I will go home tomorrow. He said, wait, and first tell Aunt Uncle so that they know what the boy would do at night. I folded my hands and said, it won't happen again. You leave me like this time; I will do whatever you say. He came to me and held my genitals with his right hand, and said,

"Then my fuck is good." I couldn't believe my ears. So I looked at him for a while. Eva Morison approached me and asked why you were staring at me. Is there force in the Penis?

I pulled her to me with a pull and said, I don't see once how to crack your pussy; I will caress you a lot. He said, you know all my girlfriends fuck with their boyfriends and come to me and talk. Mother has kept me under such control that I can't make love, who will fuck me? There is no way for him to fuck in peace.

I said it's good that you don't have a boyfriend. Then I couldn't fuck you like this. Saying this, I threw her nightie over her head. There was no reading inside. Her 32-size breasts came out like guavas in front of my eyes. Without thinking anything else, I started touching her nipples. Eva Morison started to cool comfortably.

At the same time, my Penis started shaking. My Penis became so hard that it felt like an iron rod. I sucked her breast for some time and then laid her down. She was wearing a green panty underneath. I couldn't take it anymore. I immediately took off her panty and made her completely naked. For the first time in my life, I saw a girl's pussy from the front. Clean pussy with all hairs removed.

A little swollen, so beautiful The juice comes out, and the pussy is thoroughly wet. I kissed her navel and then brought my face down to her pussy. I made a gap between the holes with my finger and inserted the jive. There is no foul smell in her vagina. I started sucking her pussy. Eva Morison now started scurrying like a slaughtered chicken. Now I put my tongue in the pussy and started licking.

Meanwhile, my Penis feels like it's going to explode. Now I sat up and took my down to her face. Eva Morison put my 6" size cock in her mouth and started sucking. I felt like I had reached heaven. Because of her sucking, my semen came out. Now I took the Penis out of her mouth and brought it near her cunt mouth. He told me, I can't do it anymore, come in now. The pussy is full of juice.

I put the head of my Penis slightly into the mouth and pressed but slipped. After two more contractions, Eva Morison held my Penis in her hand and held it in her mouth. After pushing hard, it entered the vagina. He shouted.

I stopped; what do you think? "Don't," he said, closing his eyes. Full tight pussy. My dish is under tremendous pressure. I started fucking in that situation. At first, I was fucking slow. Then I increased the speed. I put my Penis completely in the pussy and take it out again.

Eva Morison started moaning happily as I increased the speed of my fucking. I press her breast with one hand and fuck hard. After fucking like this for quite some time, my semen was about to come out. Now I brought out the Penis. Then I put him on top of him with a little kiss. This time her pussy is in front of me. Such a beautiful ass that cannot be explained.

I massaged the ass thoroughly with both hands. Then I spread the legs a little and washed the Penis in his pussy. I was enjoying this position more than before. After fucking like this for some time, I realized that it was time for both of us. This time I reduced the speed of the fuck. As Eva Morison screamed, her whole body shuddered and stopped.

As I fucked the Penis hard a few more times, the semen started to come out. I have never been out before. Eva Morison's back and ass were filled with my semen.

I cleaned the threads with her nightie and turned her towards me. He smiled and hugged me. After that, I got clean from the bathroom and hugged both of them naked. In the morning, before Uncle came, I had sex once again. That's the beginning. Since then, sometimes,

I would go to her house and have sex at my house.

Bringing Aunt's Daughter to Bed

My name is Nick Johnson.

This is my nickname. I'm a brilliant boy, and I've had sex with more strangers than I've ever had sex with girls in my life.

I don't sleep if I don't masturbate every morning, noon, and night regularly, and I don't sleep if I don't see my Bangla chatty story on this site, so I thought I would present a true story of mine to you if you like it then many more strange things happened to me which I will share with you. I will show you.

All my facts will be true, and nothing will be fictional. And the story I will tell. This is true. My uncle's daughter lives next door to my house, she is five years younger than me, now I am 28 and she is 23 in college, never noticed her. But my sister looks beautiful. My sister was noticed by many of my friends. But because of the political connections in my area, no one would dare to tell me.

Seriously, like a grandpa. used to behave, but one day everything changed due to a reason one of my friends was doing a tour travel business.

My sister and her parents went on that tour. Let's give my sister's physical identity; she is a very fair and normal figure, and her breasts are 34, and she has light belly fat.

I drink daily; for example, when they come back, I go into the house to have a drink. And they lived in the house next to mine; my sister suddenly messaged me, brother, are you at home? I said, yes,

I just came back; my friend who took them on a trip saw him with his brother's eyes, but he sat in his car, put his hand on his chest and stomach, and pressed the milk.

I was also surprised when he said these words to me during that tour while he was sleeping, and I called him every day at the hotel because he was afraid. Because the boy was not of that type. I have been excellent friends since then with my sister.

There were many close conversations, and I noticed her body but could never tell.

She used to send photos and videos in small dresses on WhatsApp status. But I used to message him when he came for a drink and try to convince him that I liked him. But she used to ignore and try to explain as if she didn't understand anything. One day,

I said in the message ok, are you a virgin and she said yes. I said I don't believe it. She said my boys don't like it, and I said that I had heck it. We started talking very closely about these. From then on, my penis was hard all the time to fuck her, sometimes when she took a bath and went home, she was only wearing a towel, and my penis would become enraptured; from then on, I would think when

I would be able to fuck her, then when she came in front of me, I would also look at the milk. Since then, I started planning every day how to get her as my own, and then, one day, luck was in my favor. My parents go to visit the village.

That day, I told him to drink alcohol, and he agreed and stayed in my room at night. We both play music, listen to TV, and drink alcohol. And both get very addicted. I asked her to show her leg tattoo, and she was shy because she didn't want to.

Then I said I gave it on Facebook, and she was not shy, so she lifted her nightly and showed it. Her addiction got stronger, and I kept touching her leg; then she said, something No, when the wine was finished, he said to lie down and put the pillow next to me, and I lay down next to him; then he took my blanket and put his feet on me.I got excited, too.

Then, I put my hand on her body and slowly put my hand on her belly button, and then she removed my hand because of intoxication. From above the nightie. Then she says what's going on? I am your sister. I will say first that I am a boy. You are a girl then, after saying any relationship, come after, come and keep pressing the milk. She doesn't say anything else.

Then I hold her and kiss her on the lips and suck her lips, and she responds.

Then she gets excited. Then slowly, I took off her nightie and pressed her breasts and gave one suck and pulled her nipples and sucked, then I put my hand inside the panty and saw that her pussy was completely wet.

I slowly put my hand in the pussy and then started fingering it with two fingers and slowly started making noises like this and then took my seven-inch penis and started lowering it.

My penis got hard. Takes my penis in front of her face, and Lakshmi starts sucking my penis up and down like a girl. Sucks my penis with good care.

Then I fuck her pussy and suck it well; she puts my head in her pussy then she gets hot and tells Bro, I can't fuck anything then.

I'm going to fuck my penis, but it's so tight that I don't want to go in.

Then, with one push, half of it goes in, then with another push, it goes all the way in and screams out loud! Ah! Ah! Ah! Ah! Ah!

She started making noises, and I got excited by her sound and started to fuck hard and spread my legs, and within a few moments, she cums and squeezes my penis in her pussy.

I lay down with my head on his chest.

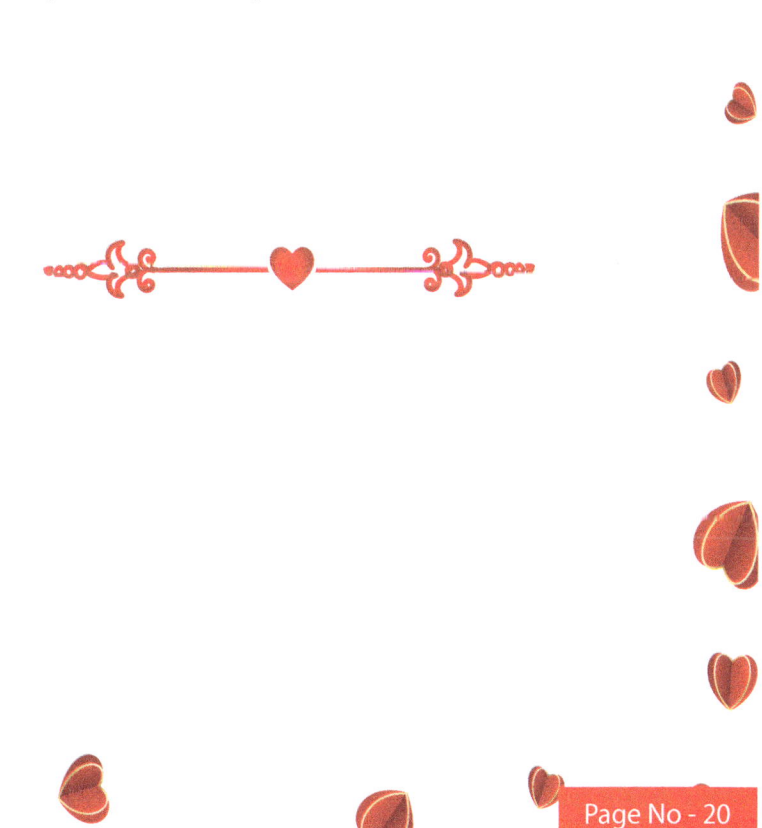

Which I Gave the Teacher Felt Extreme Happiness

Hello, friends Angelina and me. I came up with one more incident in my life, which happened to me from a college madam.

A madam named Lisa was in our department with a fair complexion, though not very fair. And the appearance was a little heavy, round fat body.

I loved Madam Madam, especially when her hair blew in the wind and fell on her face. Her figure was so heavy that if she wore leggings with selore, her lower abdomen would have been very tight. And seeing the open parts of her sweaty body would be very nice if she wore a saree.

I wanted to lick the body going to the game. But she wears a saree above the navel, which was one of my regrets. Because, as I said earlier, women's navels turn me on. I thought I would never see it.

Madam teaches well, and if anyone does not understand something, she goes to the department after the class and explains it. But even so, a depression works in him. In between, there is another mind.

I learned that her love marriage took place about 6 years ago, but her husband is away on business, and after a few months, he comes home for two or three days but continues with work. Do not give special time to Madam.

Whenever I meet Madam, I talk, and I like to talk to her, and besides, I have a crush on her. One day, I went to another place for a little need and saw that Madam was there. After I finished speaking, sir told me there was a program in an auditorium in Kolkata the next day.

Ma'am will go there, and a student can go, so if anyone wants to go, he should come immediately and give his name. I saw this as a good opportunity to spend some time with Madam, so I gave my name to go.

I will also get the attendance for that day, and there will be food and drink. I talked with the Madam about going the next day, and the phone number was also given. After some time, Madam's Whats App status is also seen, and she gives different statuses, such as love, sadness, etc.

He told me to stand at the railway station at night between 9.30 and 10 am. The next morning, I reached before 9.30 and called and learned that Madam's train would arrive at the station shortly.

After a while, I met Madam wearing a cream-colored woven saree and orange blouse; the saree was a bit transparent in the air. I could see everything inside except the navel because I had already said Madam looked incredibly beautiful. I said, "I don't recognize you today."

He smiled and said, "So?" I also smiled a little. He came and said that he had rented a car to and from the college, but if we go by bus because of the time, even if lunch is free, we can go out in the evening and eat something with that money.

I also agree with that. I talked to Madam, and she also saw Frankly talking and asked me about my house and future. Arriving at the bus stand is the responsibility of getting on the bus, which is very crowded during office hours.

We both sat down and pushed each other. There is no condition to enter inside; I am standing before me, Madam. It is hot and crowded on it. I was sweating and saw that Madam was also sweating.

The back of her blouse is cut very deep, almost up to the back, and that open part is getting wet with sweat. Uff wanted to touch. I was standing on the bus rod with my right hand, so my left hand was free.

Madame's fat folded back was exposed through the bottom of the blouse, but despite the crowd's pressure, I gently touched her back with my left hand so she wouldn't notice. I saw that the back was also sweaty.

I wish I could hug his sweaty body.

After some time, the front seat was empty, and Madam asked me to sit instead of sitting because a man in dirty clothes was sitting next to me.

After I sat down, Madam stood on my left side, hugging me under the crowd's pressure. Once, there was so much pressure that she stood on the bus rod from two sides, and her saree moved from the middle of her stomach, and her stomach came almost in front of my face.

It was such a situation that the navel would come out if the saree were lowered a little. Thus, we reached the destination. She is sweating due to the heat and crowd, and her blouse is wet.

The hair fell on her sweaty face in such a way that it looked wonderful, and her sweaty body looked very hot and sexy. Both of them took some photos inside before entering.

I felt relieved as AC was inside, and he felt some peace. The tip of his forehead was a little off, which he couldn't put in place.

I fixed it with his consent, and I could touch it slightly. We sat a little further back on the edge to wander outside if bored. I am on the side, and he is on the seat to my right. After a while, I saw that he was leaving a picture on the status.

I saw it, too. Suddenly, I saw that he was saving some hot type love status on Facebook; there was a post, "After marriage, a husband must meet the financial and emotional needs of his wife as well as her physical needs," which he edited and wrote under it "which I don't get and will get in the future."

I don't know if". When I saw it in his eyes, he smiled and locked the phone. I was curious and asked why he gave such a status.

He wanted to talk, but I assured him, "You can tell me, ma'am; I can assure you that no one will know, and you will feel a little lighter."

Then she said that she met her husband in college life. He is not such a bad person, but he doesn't give her time.

He also said they are not financially lacking; the lack is elsewhere. "So what's wrong, ma'am?" I asked incredulously. He said it could not be said this way; it had to be understood. I deliberately said,

"I don't understand" again. And I started to assure again and again. After that, he remained silent for a few seconds and sighed, saying he was not physically happy.

Her husband loved her very much after marriage; he didn't let her sleep all night on the wedding night, and even on honeymoon, he would pull her close whenever he got a chance. But gradually, physical contact between them decreases as the days go by.

Her husband is busy working from home, even when he comes home on vacation. Even after 6 years of marriage, she could not become a mother. Listening to his story, I got hot, and my device stopped inside.

Madam, to sit on my right, I saw that her breast size is quite big, her belly is quite smooth, and it would be fun if you gave her a hand.

I think if she gets fucked then it will be great fun. I wonder what can be done. Bought a maja (mango cold drink) on entry. I ate a little of it and gave it to Madam. While eating, he suddenly put a lot of milk on his breast And fell into a sari.

It was lying on the chest in such a way that it entered through the cleavage between the breasts and rolled on the stomach through the blouse, which, even if I wanted to lick it, I could not. Then he went to the washroom and washed everything with water.

After coming, I saw that the front of the saree was wet, and the stomach and chest were full of water. While sitting, I rubbed my right hand with her milk, but I didn't say anything as she didn't say anything.

I am still thinking about how to bring him closer. Although by now I have become very free with Madam. After watching some programs, we came out a bit. Even if it's hot outside, ventilating doesn't take much.

My device is tight inside, and I squeeze hard to make Madam feel a little hot.

Suddenly, one of Madam's hands touched my device, and she was slightly surprised. He smiled at me and said,

"What's the matter, Joy? What's the situation?" I said, "It's nothing, ma'am." I smiled. Then I said, "Ma'am, your husband cannot keep a good wife; even if he is lucky, he is unlucky"."

While talking, I walked and reached an empty tree with a place to sit. Sitting there, he heaved a sigh and said, "If only he understood that." A little later, he said, "Maybe this is my fate; I may have to spend the rest of my life like this without physical pleasure."

There were no people around, so I boldly stepped forward and lifted his face by his snout and removed the hair that was flying on his face with one hand, and said, "If you want, I can give you that happiness"."

He said, "That's not the case, Joy, you are my student." I said, "I may have another relationship with you inside the college, outside the college."

"But...." As he was going to say something, I pressed his face with one hand and with the fingers of the other hand, I said,

"No, but from now on, you and me." Saying this, I kissed her forehead and said, "I love you since the day I saw you." My penis was then erect and tentacle over my pants. Seeing that, he said,

"That's why this situation happened?" I said otherwise, what? Then I sat on her right side and put my left hand on her shoulder. She kept her head on my shoulder and said that she and her husband's love and affection started sitting on the grass under a tree.

I listened to him and first held him with my left hand tighter, then the hand started to go down a little. In this way, I put the hand on the left side of his stomach and the waist.

I said, "How soft and smooth your stomach is, oops," and suddenly kissed her on the lips. He said, "So soon?"

When I saw that it was time for lunch, I said, "Let's have lunch and then see what happens". After saying this, we both took the coupon, went to the lunch place, and had lunch. After lunch, I saw that many seats around our seats were empty, so I said that I would make love sitting here in AC.

Now, by making Lisa sit on my left seat, I sit on her right side and put my left hand on her stomach like before lunch. I brought a cold drink before sitting. I asked Lisa if she would eat. He said, "There is no more room in the stomach; I have eaten a lot today."

I said, "So if there is room in the stomach, remove the saree." He said, "It is uncivilized; you don't do this in public places." I said, "No one is around; no one will see." Saying this, I moved the saree over the stomach with my right hand. I rubbed my right hand on the stomach and gently caressed the stomach with my left hand.

He said, "Please don't do it; someone will see it and feel pressure in the stomach." I said, "No one will see honey, and I am reducing the pressure on the stomach."

I said, "No one will see honey, and I am reducing the pressure on the stomach." Saying this, I grabbed her saree with both hands and pulled it down below the navel. Ugh, her navel is big and deep; I feel like my penis will enter the front.

Lisa said, "If you do this, you are embarrassing me." I said, "Sit quietly; what's the shame? No one will see." After that, with the right hand around her navel and around the middle navel

I started fingering. After that, I started to rotate it inside the navel with my fingers, and I saw Lisa slowly making noises in her mouth.

After a while, he got up and went to the toilet. He returned and said, "Please, I can't take it anymore, Joy, make me cool today." I said, "But there is no such place here and no such hotel. Where do I go now?" Lisa said,

"Don't worry. My husband and I have bought a flat here; I came in between. I have brought the key today.

If I am late, I will stay here if I can't return." Go there." I also agreed to go. We took a cab and went to that flat. I didn't want to wait anymore, so I entered the flat and hugged Lisa; she said, "Wait, first turn on the AC; it's sweltering, then do what you want to do."

So I left it then. Then I pounced on her after turning on the AC in her bedroom. I hugged her from behind and opened her hair, then started to lick the open part of the back of the blouse from her neck with my mouth, and with both hands, I started pressing two milks on the blouse. He was ahh ahh in comfort.

Then I turned her forward and kissed her lips, face, and cheeks. After slowly kissing the two milk nipples on the neck over the blouse, I began to suck her entire belly with my tongue around the navel.

Then I inserted my tongue into the navel and started licking it, and she kept my head on her belly and started enjoying it. Then he grabbed Lisa thr, ew her on the bed pou, red a cold drink on her navel, and licked her for a while.

Then I left her navel and came up to her chest and excitedly tore the hook in front of her blouse and somehow extracted the milk from the bra and started sucking the nipples, and she was, ahh ah, in comfort.

Now I took off her saree and saiya and started kissing her by rubbing my fingers over her panty. Seeing his body moving, I realized that his condition was slowly deteriorating.

Then I removed her panty and started licking her pussy with my tongue, and she held my head. After licking her clitoris hard with her tongue for a while, she screamed and shook her whole body, releasing the long-term salty water on my face.

I then licked my face clean. Then Lisa took off my t-shirt and came down to lick my whole body and, with her hand, unbuttoned my pant and started sucking my penis. Phew, the relief I was getting is indescribable.

After sucking like this for 10-15 minutes, she told me, "Please cool me with your penis; I can't take it anymore."

After that, I made her lie on the bed and licked her pussy, and made her horny. It was a little tight for not having sex for a long time, so it entered a little. Then I pushed a little more complicated, and my cock went all the way in, and Lisa held me and said, "Ah ah, I'm dead."

Then I started to fuck slowly. I started to increase the speed of the fuck, and Lisa kept saying, "Ahh ahh uhh make me fuck harder. How long will I not get this pleasure"." After doing this for a while, she released her cum again, and I increased the speed of the application. After some time, I lay on the bed and put him on top of me, and inserted his penis into my vagina.

Now she started fucking herself up and down, and I was pressing her breasts. Her milk squirting while fucking looked great. After about two hours of fucking he was tired, and I was almost done too. I then took out my penis and set it on her navel and poured semen on her navel and took it from the navel, and smeared it all over her body. In this way, two days a week, we used to have sex in Lisa's flat, and I used to ejaculate inside her pussy without fear of taking Lisa's pill.

Passionate Love for Maid Abandoned by Husband

My name is Ravi. The incident that I will share today was a year ago.

My mother's physical condition is a little sour, so my father is a handyman. She used to stay in our house all day and night. She got a chance to go home 2 days in a month. Her milk is enormous.

It seems as if the blouse is about to tear. I just got the idea of sex then. Sometimes I flirt. But I don't remember ever looking at a woman with lustful eyes. But seeing Rahima (the worker's name), I was very attracted. Sometimes, I felt like I would lick all the meat of the woman once.

So, one day, my mother asked him about his family. He was telling everything, but at one point, he started crying. She said her husband left her, so she went out to work. She has only one daughter. Read that in class eight. He is working in our house to raise him.

Hearing his words, my mother wet her eyes with tears, but something else from this room was happening in my mind. Since that mage has not had sex with her husband for a long time, she will give herself to me if I give her a little cunt. I waited for the opportunity. One day, Father was going to Sajek for a week on an office tour.

So he took his mother with him. I didn't go because my exam was coming up. After my parents left, I decided to fuck Rahima today. I will force the woman today. So I bought 1 box of condoms from the market. I saw him doing his work. I went and asked him to make some tea for me. He went to the kitchen to make tea.

I knew that he did not make tea well. And something should be done about this. When he brought the tea, I gulped and threw the cup away. I said the tea was very awkward. He was terrified to see me getting angry.

He said to me softly, Brother, I can't make tea. I said you can't mean it. Do you sit and take money at our house? I saw him standing still in fear.

I told him to go and get the automaker from the cupboard, and he went to get it. I had already put it so that it would fall off if someone were careless, and that's precisely what happened.

The cooker fell and broke. I went there now. He was scared and said that I didn't do it on purpose. I said Mom, let me get you out of the job.

He heard that and hugged my leg. I said no, no. I once said that if you want to work, make me happy, and you will be fine.

At first, he said no. But when I scared him a lot, he kept quiet. Thinking it was a green signal, I picked her up and took her to my bedroom.

After putting her on the bed, I plunged her lips first, that thrill on her lips. I then slowly started squeezing some of her milk from under her armpit, and she moaned. I slowly opened all her clothes; nothing fell. So immediately, her two big breasts came out in front of me.

I pressed them for 5 minutes. Then I started sucking. I saw him closing his eyes and relaxing. I went down and buried my face in her navel and smelled it.

I now untied her dress and made her completely naked. I got utterly naked myself. I gave him my penis and told him to suck well. At first, he didn't, but then he sucked the penis like a whore.

One time, I saw him humming to himself. Then I laid her down and inserted my 8-inch long penis. He screamed in pain. And started to ah ah ah. Now I began to fuck slowly. After 5 minutes of fucking in this condition, I took her to missionary.

I started in doggy style. Then he started saying with his mouth, Ah ah ah ah, I'm going to die. Malkin, see how your son is fucking me. I think one day he will fuck you too.

I became more excited after hearing this in Odar's mouth, and the speed of the fuck increased. After another 15 minutes of continuous thrusting, I came out.

I was safe because I was wearing a condom. I have fucked him a lot since that day. When parents go out, fuck him. If I don't take my medicine, his pussy itches...!

It's been seven days since I fucked you. One day, when he was working, I suddenly jumped on him, and he couldn't control himself, so he gave me a hand. I started kissing her a lot, then took off my clothes and started fucking... Every fuck went to her bottom and at home, only the sound of gurgling through her mouth.

Ah ah ah ah ah ah ah ah ah ah Can't kill me Make me Fuck Fuck crazy I am your whore. I will be your protector forever... Ah ah louder... ah ah ah, Mom. I increased the speed of fucking after listening to her; she couldn't hold it anymore and started crying profusely.

Still mouthing, Ah ah ah ah ah ah ah..... I fucked her 5 times in a row and then it's night... One day, when my parents were at home, I heard my mother humming at night and realized that my parents were playing a game.

Hearing those words, my penis got hard. I went to his room.

He got scared seeing me, But I didn't hear a word. I just opened everything and filled my thick cock in her pussy... What women do sex…

Even after eating my cock, his hunger did not decrease. It also happened that I fucked her continuously for 10 hours with little rest…

That's not to stop women. That night I started to fuck her harder. I fuck, and she grunts. It seemed to hear the word, Ah ah ah ah ah ah ah on his face.

Hearing my sex increased. I keep on fucking him harder, he starts taking my cocks, and he starts fucking me from below…

Fuck her so much that she screams. Hearing that sound, Mom and Dad started coming.

Hearing Mom and Dad coming, I hid under the bed. He comes and asks what happened. He says he saw a cockroach. Parents leave.

I don't like interruptions during sex. I pressed her face and started kissing her. What a cocky cock he is…..

From his mouth only comes out, Ah ah ah ah ah ah ah ah loud fuck hit me Fuck harder You feel good because my hand was covering his face and his parents did not hear anything from the house.

And 20 minutes after I put him down, I took out the material and put him on the bed, and he came to my room and slept...

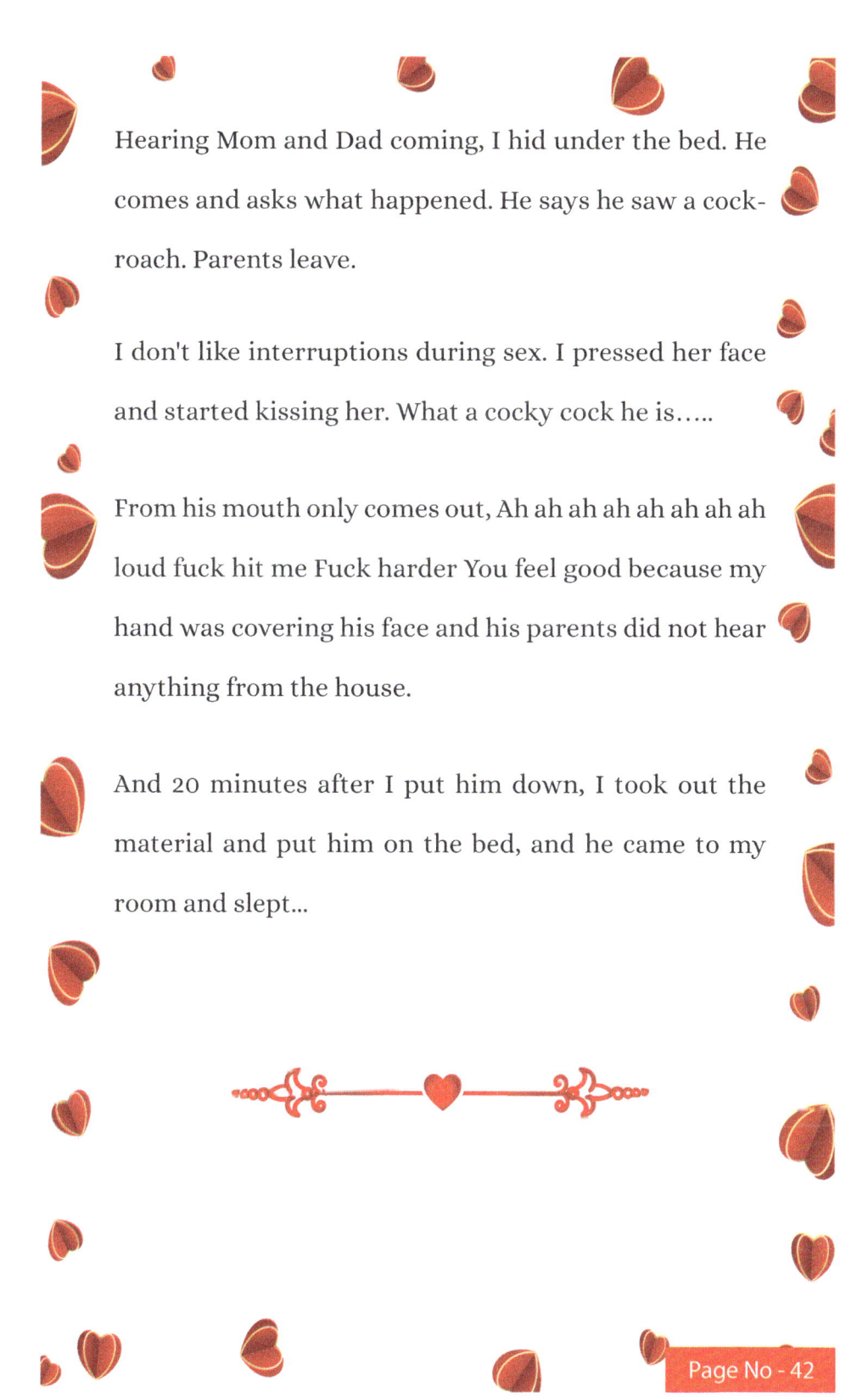

Love with Tenant Aunty

Waking up in the morning, the only thing I do these days is brush my teeth and watch my new tenant's aunty big breasts.

When Aunty bends down to wash the dishes, her buttocks are about to burst out of the nightie. Moreover, Aunty's heavy breasts, evident in her half-wet nightie and occasional red hair peeking out from her armpits while fixing her hair, never let me take my eyes off her.

Ever since the day we got home, all my meditations and desires have been all about the new tenant, Aunty. These days, I masturbate only imagining Aunty. There is no limit to how many ways I have imagined having sex with my aunt till today. I am very jealous of Aunty's husband, who means my uncle. A black man.

Full face beard and mustache. He suffers from Aunty every day. When he returns from the office, he calls Aunty daily but cannot find her at home. It seems that you are not alone, then.

I have developed a good relationship with Aunty. Sometimes, there are many stories about him. But I still could not proceed with the real matter.

Meanwhile, my desire for Aunty reached the last limit of endurance. This time, it is not necessary to do nothing. I never thought that something like this would happen in my life.

Everyone in the house went out of town for a few days for my cousin's wedding. I didn't go because my final-year exams were ahead of me. On the day when everyone left, I stepped in front of my aunt's house at night.

It was my long-time curiosity to see Aunty and Uncle fornication. As I went a little further, I heard Aunty's screams. I understand that the uncle is teasing the aunt very well.

But after a while, all the noise stopped. I heard Aunty say, "You can't fuck well today, so you have to attack so much every day.

"Hearing this, the uncle shouted, "Prostitute, you like to fuck a lot; that's why you couldn't give me a child till today." Then I heard the sound of slapping. I heard Aunty crying. I got upset and went straight upstairs to my room.

I could not accept this brutal torture on Aunty. I wanted to run away with Aunty. Aunty and I will start a new family there. I will give Aunty a lot of sexual pleasure every day. I will fill the baby in Aunty's stomach. I don't know.

When I fell asleep thinking about these reverses, I woke up in the morning and called my uncle. Seeing him, there is no way to understand why he brutally tortured his wife the night before. He told me gently that he was going out for office work for a few days and that I should see my aunt.

Aunty used to come to sleep with my mother when my uncle went somewhere. Because Aunty is afraid to be alone at night. But today, there is no one in the house except me. So Auntie, if she wanted to sleep at night, she had to sleep with me. Thinking about this, her mind started dancing with joy.

After my uncle left, I went straight to Aunty's room. I don't know when the time passed while talking and watching TV; we sat together at night to eat.

After the meal, I started to rush to my room. I wanted Aunty to ask me to stay in her room by herself. Seeing me go, Aunty said, "Where are you going, don't sleep with me tonight"? After listening to my aunt, I felt a little shy, so my aunt laughed and said, "Are you ashamed or not?"

You look at me every morning while washing the dishes; you are not ashamed! Or are you running away because you don't have the guts to fuck like my husband?"

Aunty's words directly hit my manhood. I took Aunty to her bed and whispered, "I will know if I have breath tonight." I'm not like your groom, who will kiss you for a moment. I will shake your bed all night and make you pregnant".

Saying this, I put my lips on Aunty's lips without giving her a chance to speak. It didn't take me long to open Aunty's red nightie.

I saw her nipples standing firm. I started sucking her breast milk in turn. Aunty "Ah ah ah ah! Ah ah ah ah!" He was enjoying himself. As I lifted Aunty's hands, I smelled the feminine sweat of her armpits.

I inserted my tongue in her armpit and. I felt the heavenly pleasure of licking the armpits full of khaki chemo hair. Then I reached Aunty's navel and her pussy. I got a salty taste on my tongue.

I started sipping the juice from her hairy pussy. Aunty was holding my head in her pussy and was screaming. Cuckoo's chattering and chilling increased my lust. I kept licking her pussy like crazy. At last, Aunty released her cum in my mouth, and I licked it like nectar.

Then I gave my penis in Aunty's hand and said, "Give my son a little caress, and then I will give you a lot of happiness". Aunty started pinching my penis with her hand.

Then, at one point, he ran it in his mouth. I was holding the pillow with both hands and enjoying sucking my penis.

Aunty was gently pinching my penis now and then while sucking. Happily, my eyes were closed when I woke up.

"Ah!!!" A sound of relief came out of my mouth. I started pounding Aunty little by little. The warmth of my aunt's tongue was transmitted through my cock, making my body tingle.

Not realizing that I can't hold on for much longer if this continues, I pulled my cock away from my aunt. There is still a lot of pleasure to be given to Aunty, so to ejaculate at this moment, I didn't want to.

After that, I put my penis straight in Aunty's vagina. My cock went all the way into the juicy cunt very quickly.

I started pounding Aunty hard. Shaking the bed with every stroke, I started thrusting Aunty, and she was floating in the sea of happiness, sinking my every stroke into her soft flesh.

"Ahh", "Ahh" Auntie's screams were increasing as her breathing became heavy as my Joan Pennies attacked.

I was alternately sucking Aunty's hard milk nipples. We are lonely because of such constant flirtation. But I had no intention of stopping. Constantly and increasingly, I started to fuck Aunty.

At last, he bit my neck, sensing his anger imminent. And I couldn't hold back and ejaculated in aunty with great speed. Aunty's vagina got wet with my cum. I pulled out my penis from Aunty's body.

Aunty "Ahhhh!!" made it. I noticed that even after ejaculating so much, my penis was a little dull. I understood that he wanted to enter Aunty's body once again. I changed position without delay.

Aunty looked at me questioningly. Without saying anything, I pushed my cock soaked in Aunty's cum into her anus. Aunty shouted, "Ah! It takes gold to come."

I was not in the mood to hear all this. I can't count how many times I masturbated with my imagination like this.

Today, I went crazy on the verge of making my dream come true. Grabbing a fistful of Aunty's hair, I pushed my penis into Aunty's soft ass. I whispered in Auntie's ear, "Look, don't do it." You wanted me tonight, and now I must give you all the happiness".

Aunty understood and told me it would be no use as I was not in a listening state. So he kept quiet. I started pounding Aunty's ass. I looked forward to feeling every inch of this most secret tunnel of Aunty's body. One of me rubbing aunt's anus with my cock. A different feeling was emerging.

Tightening my grip on Aunty's hair, I increased the speed of the tap. Auntie was clutching the pillow and screaming. The soft flesh of Aunty's anus was constantly pressed on my penis. I could not bear the pleasure and let my hot sperm chirp in her ass.

After winning Aunty's anus, we both got tired and lay down hugging each other. . In response, a tired body is more likely to sleep. It's not too late.

When I woke up, I saw that Kaki was still sleeping. Aunty's naked body looked beautiful in the morning light. I slowly got hard. Aunty's arms were on her head; her armpits were fully exposed.

His armpit hair was blowing randomly in the wind of the fan. I buried my face in his armpit. I smelled a light sweat. After spending some time in the armpits, I came up on Aunty.

Aunty woke up to suck milk from me. On that side, my hard penis was hitting Aunty's pussy face. Who said in a sleepy voice, "Saturday starts again...ah!!" Aunty didn't finish my cock hard and entered Aunty's cunt, waking all her sleep. Aunty said slightly pleadingly, "Well, I've gone crazy." Just going to fuck from the night.

Tell me, are you human? I said, "Honey, to you, I am just an instrument of your happiness." Auntie frowned and smiled. I also started to tap without further talking.

This is the beginning of a new relationship between us that is based on the original and genuine desire of men and women for each other - sexual desire.

From then on, I used to fuck my aunt whenever I got a chance. Never used contraception during intercourse with Aunty.

I always wanted my cum to go into Aunty's body. One day, my hard work paid off.

Uncle came into our house one day with a packet of sweets and informed us that Malvika would be Auntie Ma.

For the first time, I felt the joy of being a father.

The First Happiness of The New Year

I was promoted as soon as the new year started, but again, I had to go to another city for three months. I got a flat for three months with the help of senior staff. But the problem is the workers, so I decided to take a full-time worker from here.

As a result of contacting a nanny center in the neighborhood, they gave someone's phone number a few days ago. Name Ramla, widow, no one at home, so she has no problem going with me to another city for three months. I came to the nanny center with some advance money and called Ramla.

I called and told them to meet today at noon to shop. Ramla's voice on the phone felt somewhat familiar. Having lunch at noon, I am waiting for Ramla at the auto stand; suddenly, I see an aunty from my neighborhood coming.

Despite her age, she has a good figure, and her body has not decreased yet; she has been running the family for ten years after her husband's death, and she has wanted to fuck her aunt many times after seeing her body.

Still, she has not had the opportunity to bond with her before. So Aunty saw me and asked, "Hey baby, where are you going?" I replied, "I'm going to the lake market for a while.

Someone is supposed to come, so I'm waiting." Aunty heard and said, "I will also go to the lake market, then let's go together."

We talked for a while. While talking, I noticed Aunty's body well. Aunty is wearing a white printed saree with a light blue blouse.

The milk is quite large. Aunty looks pretty, too. After talking for a while, seeing that Ramla was not coming, I called her. At the same time, Aunty's phone rang. Auntie answered the phone and realized we were waiting for both of us.

This mistake was due to not knowing Aunty's name and not knowing that Aunty does such work. As there was no auto in the afternoon, I explained to Aunty what to do, except that I wanted to fuck her.

We became quite close as we talked. Finally, the wait was over; an auto came. Aunty got in first, and then me. While going in the auto, I touched Aunty's stomach from behind with my right hand.

It was difficult to shake hands completely, so Aunty moved towards me and facilitated me. I slowly moved my hand from the stomach to the milk and put a little pressure on it.

Aunty gently pressed my penis and put her face near my ear, and said go to the lake and give me your hand. I bought the daily necessities from the lake market and asked Aunty what to buy for you.

When Aunty didn't reply, I went to buy two hot-looking nighties for Aunty and said that you would wear them at night when you stayed with me in other cities.

Aunty said I can understand how long you will let them stay on me, and I don't have to spend so much money for ten minutes.

Aunty didn't let me buy two nighties, so I bought one, and then I bought Aunty a saree. Aunty was pleased. After shopping, I went to the lake with my aunty and sat in an empty spot.

After talking for a while, when the evening fell, we sat closer. Aunty was sitting on my left. Ramla put her right hand on my shoulder, and I hugged her. I started gently pressing my right hand on her left breast. Ramla's lips are pretty.

I started kissing Ramla without saying anything. Aunty is also responding well. I now opened two hooks of her blouse and tried to touch her breast milk from inside, but my hands could not reach the milk as I was wearing a bra.

While Ramla was wearing a brassiere, she took her left hand from it and gave it to me. I was happily kissing her breasts.

But hearing a little commotion in the distance, we left each other and sat down. Ramla said, "Nick Jhonson, go home; it is wrong to do these things here."

Leaving the lake, we took an Uber to Ramla's house. On the street, I slowly persuaded Ramla to have sex. It took us half past six to reach his house.

In one room, I requested Ramla to wear the nightie once. She turned back in front of me, took off her saree and blouse, and put on the nightie. Purushanga stood up, seeing Ramla's fair back in the room's light.

Aunt turned to me and asked, how do I feel? The white bra and the dark navy blue nightie looked very inappropriate.

I asked Aunty to remove the dress and bra. Aunty opened their bra and dress and told me it was ok now. Aunty looked good. Even at the age of 52 years, no working aunty can have such a good body.

Even at this age, the milk of 36 sizes has not hung much, the nipples are medium-sized and beautifully round,

there is little fat in the stomach, and the navel is also quite deep. Their big butt is quite round and high. I was sitting on the bed, and Aunty came and lay beside me.

I jumped on Aunty and started kissing her on the lips. While kissing, I rolled up the nightie from under Aunty's legs and pulled it on her stomach.

I saw that the vagina was full of hair with my hand, and I realized that the vagina was wet with semen.

I got down from the bed too, took off my pants too, took Aunty's hand, and brought her to the edge of the bed. Ramla still hasn't seen my penny.

I rubbed the penis in the mouth of the pussy, Ramla spread her legs further. By inserting a little bit of the penis into the opening of the vagina, a lot of the penis entered Ramla's vagina.

Even though the groom is dead, Ramla's pussy is still in good use.

At this age, no one can take my long and thick cock without making a sound.

Without thinking much, I started to fuck. Aunty herself, in that situation, took off the nightie and became full length too,k both my hands and gave her breast milk to both of them.

I continued to squeeze the milk well. Ramla holds her face with one hand and muffles the whistling sound while the other hand is holding my hand tightly. I pressed the milk and made it red.

After a long time of fucking, I still haven't got any hot cum, it seems like I can fuck well. Now I put my aunty in Doggy position to give my best fuck, and I rammed my penis in Ramla's pussy from behind.

Now I started to fuck both Ramla's ass. As I thought, after 10 minutes of loud fucking, my material will come out. In this situation, Ramla pressed her pussy to my penis and buried her face in the pillow and screamed.

I also squeezed the penis and threw all the semen into Ramla's pussy.

After some time, I took the cock out of Ramla's pussy, and some of her cum came out on the bed, and some got on my penis.

I got off the bed and stood on the floor. Ramla also got down from the bed and sat in front of me and licked the penis clean, and started sucking again.

Ramla likes testing my penis very well and knows how to suck well. I couldn't understand that this woman was a total fucking whore. I grabbed a handful of Ramla's hair and continued to fuck inside her mouth. After a while, I realized that semen would come out.

I told Ramla I would come out now. Will you take it? Aunty said that I had not eaten anyone's semen for a long time so that I would eat the whole semen. I poured some more juice into Ramla's mouth, and Aunty was satisfied with the juice.

After eating Aunty's juice, I lay on the bed, and Aunty lay beside me. Aunty asked me if I was happy. I said when did you fuck before? You can fuck and relax well, even at this age.

Aunty told me that before I got a job, I worked as a woman's nanny for one and a half years, then her son would fuck aunty every night when the woman slept, but four months after the boy's marriage, aunty quit that job.

These four months, Aunt Gud has not eaten anyone's pussy. Aunty said, "You may give me less, but please kiss me twice daily." I assured Aunty that I would satisfy the hunger of Aunty's body. As I lay awake, Ramla climbed on top of me again and started foreplay.

I enjoyed it, too. Until now, I used to warm everyone before; today, someone is warming me up, saying that they will fuck. As soon as my penis was erect, Ramla sucked it and took it in a cowgirl pose.

Aunty continued to fuck from above for quite some time, I was also fucking from below, but I don't know why my juice doesn't come out easily in cowgirl pose.

After about 20 minutes of sex, Ramla got off of me once with cum. I asked Ramla to hold the wood of the window and hold her pussy up.

Ramla's ass is big, like a jug. Lubricant must beat the ass. As it was winter, there was Vaseline body lotion in the house. I worked with that. Kakima had never fucked her ass before; the boy tried but couldn't, said Aunty.

Naturally, Aunty's butt was tiny. After five minutes of effort, I managed to insert my penis into Ramla's ass.

But this time, it was a little difficult for Ramla to take my penis in the ass. Aunty's hot ass made my cock even more excited.

Now, I asked Ramla to leave the window's wood and take the edge of the bed. As a result, the butt became higher.

I licked my breasts and fucked my ass well, and let out my cum in my ass. I saw that Ramla was a little lame. I will not fuck today.

I am also tired. I booked food online. Aunty put on the nightie, and I put on all the clothes and pants. Tomorrow night train. I told Aunty to arrange everything.

After a while, the food was served. We had dinner together. Before coming home, Ramla sat on my lap and gave me a deep lip kiss, and asked me to suck her milk.

I put Ramla on the bed and sucked her 36-size breasts well. My penis got hard again after sucking, so I fucked Ramla well again.

I threw everything in Ramla's mouth. Before coming home, Ramla said, "Will you be here every day starting tomorrow?"

I said, "Let's go to another city first and then see how I can fuck".

Mother Fucks Uncle

Father has been very busy since this morning; when Mother asked him why he was busy, Father said,

"Today, after 15 years, my elder brother will come from London; he didn't even come to my wedding when he heard that my son had grown up, so to see him and meet you. Will come for two days, but…"

"But what?" Mom asked, "I have important work Today; I can't stay home. I will leave tomorrow morning, so I must care for my elder brother Today." "Don't worry, I will take care of your brother."

Uncle arrived home this afternoon. Uncle is very tall, but his complexion is black. Today is my holiday, so I am home.

Mother is very well dressed because my uncle is coming home for the first time. Mom is already very sexy, age 38, with fair skin like milk and red lips.

The most attractive mother's big breasts, soft balloon-like breasts, are so big that they will come out by pushing the blouse.

From the beginning, the uncle is watching the mother's milk in such a way that if he gets it in his hand, he will suck it and eat it.

As the mother bent to bow, she began to take a good look at the folds of the mother's chest. No matter how much the uncle said "Bouma Bouma" from the front, his mind started to suck his mother from inside.

Uncle's wish came true in the evening. Mother took a bath this evening due to extreme heat. After the bath, a yellow saree fell, and a black bra and shaya could be seen.

Sometimes, mothers don't wear blouses, only a bra so that breast milk can be seen from the inside.

This form of mother looks more sexy. Uncle was sitting on the sofa watching TV. I was reading in my room. I suddenly realized that I had to go to my mother.

Opening the door lightly, I saw Mother leaning before Uncle, giving him breakfast.

Suddenly, Uncle began to rub his hands on Mother's back, then pressed her ass; when Mother wanted to come away angrily, Uncle held her and said,

"I want to suck you once, just once." Mother stood silent. No words come out of Mother's mouth. I closed the door and looked through the light gap.

Uncle began to kiss Mother's neck with his black lips; Mother said, "Look, my son will come." Uncle said, "Don't come." "What are you doing, my big brother?"

"You have to listen to the elders, dear girl, don't take it once, what's the problem? The mind that is dying to drink your milk." Mother was silent now, face lowered, and said, "Hurry, what you do?"

Uncle removed the hem of the saree from the mother's chest, then put his hand inside the bra and began to squeeze the milk like flour.

Between his black lips, mother's red soft fluffy lips and began to suck. He took out the mother's milk from the bra and started sucking it as if he would eat all the milk.

After that, the mother's sai untied the rope and stripped her naked. When Mother sat down, Uncle took out his long black penis and held it in front of Mother's face; Mother smiled in surprise and said,

"You have such a big black penis?" So he put it in his mouth and kept sucking it like a lollipop. After 3 minutes, Uncle poured his hot white cum into mom'sMom's mouth.

Hot cum mother licked, said to uncle "Ah, I can't do it anymore, Dinna put that long black pen inside my pussy, I didn't want to be fucked by someone again and again, today after a long time, my body is happy after drinking someone else's hot cum, don't come"

Uncle said, "Honey, today I will fuck you and crack your pussy." Then uncle put his mouth between mother's legs, inside the pussy and started licking,

mother started to "ah ah" with satisfaction. After some time, my semen came out. Today, I realized that mom inside is crazy for this kind of sex. Mother lay down on the floor, and Uncle's stiff cock stood stiffly upright.

After that, Mother Uncle's cock came into her pussy and screamed, "Ahhhhhh" Uncle pushed his penis inside Mom's pussy, then Mom started sitting up and making noises like "Ahh ugh, mum." Then began the Dogging Style; with mom on her knees like a dog, uncle started fucking mom's pussy, cracking mom's pussy loudly, and my gentle mom was screaming, "Ahhhhhhh, ugh, ah, um, louder.".

Uncle started thrusting his black penis harder and harder into his mother's red pussy. In this way, I masturbated after watching my mother and uncle fuck. My mother's body and I got a little intoxicated; I thought Today, I will press the milk while sleeping next to my mother. but, That night, Mom didn't sleep near me, and I realized Uncle's long black penis made Mom crazy.

My Child in The Maid's Woman

I have not given my name for the sake of anonymity. My current age is 32 years. The incident happened 5 years ago when I was 27 years old. I am a doctor and dermatologist by profession. I am a village boy.

After my parents died, I survived everything. I bought a flat in the town and started living there. Where I used to live, I had an aunt to work. But when I came to a new place, I encountered a problem. Even after a week, I am not getting any workers.

A 45-year-old girl works in the flat next door. Even after telling him a lot, he did not agree. She said she is already doing two homework assignments and needs help to take up new work.

I said to contact him if there is anyone else. Two days later, at eight o'clock in the night,

I was sitting in the drawing room watching TV and suddenly the calling bell rang. Open the door and see the work aunt. There is another girl with him.

The aunt said Father said, you need a helper, so I brought Alessa. He needs a job. But there is a condition. I asked what condition. He has no place to stay if you let him stay here.

I said, no, no, how come? Before the word was finished, Alessa hugged my legs and started crying. I somehow managed to outrun Manti. I asked why are you crying like this. Aunt said she was barren, and that's why her husband threw her out of the house.

Now she has nowhere to go; if you show some mercy, then the girl will survive.

Hearing such a sad story, I could not say no. I asked you to bring some things with you.

He did not say he was kicked out of the house in one piece of cloth. Then I let Manti into the flat and closed the door.

My flat is big enough: four rooms, two bedrooms, one kitchen. A small servant room. Anyway, let me give you a little description of Alessa's body.

Minti is 25 years old, has a height of five feet, a dark body color, a thin body, and nothing to say milk; the body is so thin that it looks like someone wrapped clothes around a banana tree.

So, although the facial structure is reasonable, Alessa cannot be called Ms due to her physical structure.

I looked at the clock, and it was half past eight. I told Alessa everything was in the kitchen: go and cook for both of us.

I will come soon. Saying this, I went out. I returned after an hour. The girl came wearing a very old saree. The saree that was falling was also torn in places.

So from the outside, two saree blouses for the girl and four pairs of bra panty sets. I gave them to Alessa's hand and told her to take a bath and change her clothes.

Some tears in the girl's eyes. I growled that I wouldn't say I liked crying at all. To stay here, I had to be happy. Take a bath, eat and sleep.

The food was placed on the dining table. I ate and fell asleep in my room. I woke up at eight o'clock. After nine o'clock, I freshened up and went to the chamber. I came back at noon.

I was surprised when I went to the flat. The girl has arranged and made the whole flat beautiful. I am happy and praise Alessa. Alessa says this is her job.

After having lunch, I went out again, and while leaving, I gave some money to a beggar and said if you have any shopping, buy it. I will be back in the evening. I came back at seven o'clock. Alessa then imposed the night cooking.

I bathed, sat on the sofa, turned on the TV, and asked Alessa to bring tea. Raising the cup of tea with one hand. On the other hand, Alessa's pussy itched once.

I woke up in the morning and saw what Alessa was doing and itchy pussy with one hand.

As I doubted the matter, I told Alessa without pretense. Why are you itching there? If there is any problem, you can tell me. Alessa lowered her face in shame. I said I'm a dermatologist, so if there's a problem, there's no shame in saying it.

Alessa said yes, brother. I mean, it is a little itchy. I said okay, come out. I am watching. Alessa kept her face down without saying a word, I said. No shame, I'm a doctor, and if it's itchy, it can be contagious.

Then I took Alessa's hand and asked me to sit on the sofa and show her the clothes. As soon as she lifted her saree, Alessa's hairy vagina came out.

I said if it is filled with so much hair, it will be itchy there. You can't see anything with so much hair. Cut it and keep it clean. I'll check back in the evening.

After saying this, I finished eating and went to the chamber. I came back at seven o'clock. Then, while I was sitting on the sofa, Alessa brought tea.

Alessa nodded yes when asked if the pubic hair was cut. Then, I asked Alessa to sit at the dining table. When Alessa picked up her clothes, I pulled the chair and sat in front of Alessa's pussy.

The shaved pussy looks like the pussy of a young girl who has just gone through puberty. Although Alessa is a married 25-year-old young woman, the pussy looks like it has not been fucked by anyone and remains as it was.

Suddenly, my begging words cut off my dizziness. What are you seeing like this, brother? Did you understand something? I said the disease is prevalent because you and I can solve this disease.

Alessa said what happened to me. I said directly without pretending. when was the last time you released your semen? Alessa did not answer.

Alessa said my husband is a drunkard. Every night, he comes home drinking. We could never have sex. He started crying after 5 minutes in full bed at night.

I said to Alessa, you have got an infection due to the vaginal discharge around your vagina. Insert your fingers into the vagina regularly and remove the vagina.

Always keep the vagina clean. Everything will be fine in a few days. Alessa was surprised…… the girl did not know about fingering. The girl is very raw about sex.

I said, I will show. Saying this, I put Alessa on the dining table. Then I folded my knees, spread my legs, and lifted the saree to my waist.

Alessa's whole body trembled as soon as my fingertip touched Alessa's cunt. Then I took a little spit in my hand and started spitting on the beggar's pussy.

Alessa closed her eyes. As soon as I inserted a part of my fingertip into the vagina, I realized that there was a fire burning inside the vagina.

I slowly inserted a finger into Alessa's pussy. Alessa closed her eyes and started breathing heavily. Inserting a finger.

I realized that the pussy was very tight, begging that what he said was right; he hadn't had a cock in it for a long time. After 2-4 times fingertip, the juice started gushing out from the beggar's cunt.

Alessa also began to fuck his fingers inside the pussy to make it twist like a snake. He pleaded loudly. How much better it would have been if you had known the pleasure of inserting your finger. Brother, insert it more strongly.

I feel perfect. I started inserting my fingers at high speed, and Alessa also got quiet by twisting her body and letting out all the juice. Meanwhile, my penis was erect inside the lungi.

Alessa is looking at my penis in surprise. Alessa asked me brother can I have a little look at your cock. My 9-inch long three-inch thick penis came out to lift my Dress.

Alessa was shocked to see such a big penis. Alessa said her husband's penis is not bigger than 5 inches. She never dreamed that the penis would be so big.

Alessa said if such a big penis enters my vagina, I will die. I am a doctor, so I have to see a lot of girls' pussy. I didn't even think about begging. But listening to Alessa's words, it seemed that she wanted to fuck me.

Do not want or why a 25-year-old young woman did not get the happiness of having a husband. A penny like that in front of the eyes, no girl can be okay.

I said nothing would happen. Saying this, I stood up, pulled Alessa, and lifted Alessa's legs on my shoulder. I picked up a glass of white blood on the dining table and smeared it on my penis.

Alessa's cunt has just come out, so the cunt is very slippery. But still, Alessa's pussy is like a baby pussy. Set the head of the penis in the vagina and gently press the head to insert it. Alessa cried out, saying Babago.

I started pressing the milk slowly. Her small, thin body could not move under my 6-foot body. After lying helplessly for five minutes, Alessa also began to respond.

I understand that the girl's butt pain is over, and now she is ready for sex.

I slowly started to fuck. The chanting of the beggars gradually began to turn into a chill. Uh, Ah Ah Ah Ah, While making these sounds, he was hugging my maja with both legs so that I couldn't fuck properly.

So I sat up and lifted Alessa's legs on my shoulder and started to fuck her. Alessa also closed her eyes, held the sheet, and continued to fuck me.

I have fucked many girls with money, but I never got the pleasure I am getting today in Alessa's tight pussy. Meanwhile, Manti started twisting her body twice, three times. I understand that his time has come. So I increased the speed of the fuck.

Suddenly, Alessa jumped like a cut fish and dropped the water. My cock could no longer hold the material after being touched by the hot juice of Alessa.

I ejaculated inside the vagina. Then I lay down next to Alessa, and we both yawned. After a while, Alessa said my pussy is burning; the girl's pussy is cracked due to my big penis fucking.

I gave him a pain medicine. I did not kiss the girl that day. In the morning, I woke up suddenly feeling the tip of the penis, lifting my lungi and begging to suck my penis like a lollipop.

As a result of sucking like that, I could no longer hold the penis. I filled Alessa's mouth with sticky semen. Alessa also saw that he had eaten all the semen. My penis drooped after ejaculation.

Alessa said with a smile, get up. It's morning. After ejaculating on Alessa's face, now the body feels very hot. I was going to read the Dress, but Alessa said what would happen again after the Dress.

Now I have two animals in the flat. After leaving the room, I hugged her from behind and kissed her neck. I filled the armpit with my hand and started pressing two small milks.

Meanwhile, my Penis Babaji stood up and started thrusting near Alessa's ass. Alessa also closed her eyes in bliss. He put his body on mine.

I spread Alessa's leg a little and applied my cock's spit from behind, inserted my cock into Alessa's pussy from behind, and started fucking. Alessa's pussy was full of orgasms, and my penis moved inside.

Beg and plead as my fuck speeds up. Oof, ah, father, mother, what happiness are you giving, brother? Saying these things, I started to scream.

My flat had little furniture, and the sound of begging made the entire room a frenzy. I stood like this for 10 minutes and ejaculated inside Alessa's pussy.

Then Alessa walked to the kitchen. I entered the bathroom and took a bath. Then I went to the office after eating. I didn't come to eat at noon because I was very stressed that day.

I said to Alessa. Keep the pussy ready, and I will fuck you all night. Alessa says hundreds of insects are buzzing inside my pussy to eat your fuck.

You don't delay much. A month I was passed like this. Alessa's body has changed a lot in this one month. The thin body has become a little fatter than before. And the size of the milk is now bigger than before.

Why not? If the girls' bodies are appropriately fucked, then it doesn't take long for the body to get heavy. It was Sunday. I was sitting on the couch with my legs spread. My lungi is up to my waist

Manti sat on my lap and fucked hard by inserting the hard penis inside her pussy. Suddenly, the call rang. We were both shocked that no one came to our flat.

Alessa got up and went to open the door while reading the nightie next to her. I also took off my lungi. The hard penis was visible from inside the Dress, so I put a pillow on my lap.

I opened the door and said you!!!! What are you doing here? What do you need here? I got up and went to the door to see a stranger. The man saw me and bowed hands and said Alessa husband.

Come and say what I said. Then the man locked the door to come inside. I sat on the sofa, and the man sat on the floor. He folded his hands and told me I had come to take my wife back, and I realized my mistake.

Tell me what to do, doctor, and like five other people, I wanted to be a father. I thought that the wife was tied, so she could not handle the anger in her head.

I beat him and threw him out of the house. But when I learned that the problem was mine, what was the use of hurting the girl?

I said this is a matter of your private family, and I don't want to say anything about it.

If your wife agrees, you can take her if you wish. Alessa did not agree to go with him. Finally, I said okay, you go home today.

I will explain Manti at night. Alessa's husband got upset with my words and was preparing to leave. I said tomorrow morning, you bring your semen in a vial.

I want to test to see if you can ever become a father. As he left happily, Alessaeyes started to water. The girl is really into sex. She can't stay without sex for a day.

That day I took Viagra and fucked the girl for the whole night. I explained that she can fuck me whenever she wants and how will she spend her entire life if she doesn't have her husband's family.

Finally, he said okay, then give me a child.

I want your child to be born in my womb. I smiled to myself; I had already done that trick.

In the morning, Alessa husband took Alessa with the vial of semen. They left. I threw the vial in the dustbin. I called Minute's husband to the office.

Then I gave him an antibiotic and told him to take it, eat it right away, and keep on fucking his wife.

After a month, you will get happy news. The man believed me and did so. After a month, Alessa and her husband met me in my chamber with sweets.

Alessa and I both laugh because we both know whose baby it is.

Arpa's Sexual Desire

My name is Soumya. I will tell the story about my younger sister Arpa and my friend Shakib. Some background is the beginning of the event.

My father is an engineer in a private firm, and my mother is a homemaker; we are two siblings, Soumya and my younger sister Arpa, who is in class 12. I am in my second year of college, and my friend Shakib is also studying at the same college as me.

My sister Arpa looks pretty dark-skinned, but her figure is Jose! Because of this figure, she is widely known and often looked at with lustful eyes by all the men in the neighborhood.

No one else has such a full chest and such a big ass at such a young age. Arpa also understood this very well and always presented himself as such; for example, after taking a bath, he would always wear tight clothes and go to the roof without a veil, and the Bodinga boys would enjoy it from the roof of the neighboring house.

Arpa also enjoyed this but did not do much in public. So everything was going like this. Meanwhile, Shakib is known as my very close friend.

He had free access to my house, although I did not know him for long. Shakib could easily manipulate people's minds and was a bit of a sly type. Shakib had many girlfriends, almost all of whom Shaqib had sex with, and he also showed me pictures of some of his x gf.

He is a master at getting girls to have sex very quickly. I was a bit jealous of him for that. On the first day, when I realized the incident, I woke up around 10:30 a.m. and bathed.

Shakib was supposed to come to my house around 11 a.m., but there was some work on college lab notes. Dad left for the office early in the morning, and Mom was out on an urgent errand.

Only my younger sister Arpa and I were at home. I was showering when I heard the bell ringing. I realized Shakib had come.

So I hurriedly finished my shower in five to seven minutes and went out of the bathroom; my nature is to do almost everything silently so that Shakib and Arpa didn't hear me open the door.

As usual, I slowly walked towards the drawing-room, and then, through the gap in the curtain, I saw Shakib kissing my sister and squeezing her milk; I was surprised. What is happening? I am still quiet by nature. I watched for some more time.

I saw Shakib slowly putting his hand inside Arpa's shirt and squeezing the milk. Arpa is no less. She slips her hand inside Shakib's pant chain.

For a while, I thought, let's see how far the matter has gone. So I quietly backed into the bathroom again, my penis got hard, so I masturbated.

Now, I took out the goods and opened the door loudly so that they would know that I was leaving and so that they would not know that I knew about it. Coming out of the bathroom, I walk towards the drawing room with sandals on my feet.

Arpa comes out of the drawing room. He saw me and said, "Sakib brother has come." So Arpa went to her room and locked the door.

When he entered the drawing room, Shakib said, "Hey, dude, it takes so long to shower! Wait, dude, I'm going to the bathroom, Hebi said." I said, "Okay, go." I understand Shakib will go to the bathroom and handle the goods.

Shakib left after I finished my work, and Arpa didn't talk to me. Arpa went to my aunt's house with her mother in the afternoon. Arpa left her mobile phone. I checked her mobile phone out of curiosity! Shakib did not leave my sister. He is playing Jabbar!

I read their Facebook conversation for about fifteen hours. Filled with nude pictures of Arpa, sometimes Shakib's hard penis is also seen! They are sexting in extreme rage. Seeing my sister's figure, I started to get greedy.

I saw 3 times maal masturbating karram orpa nude pictures. I also saw his night video conversation with Shakib.

I understand that the water has flowed far. After reading the conversations, I learned that Shakib offered Arpa to rent a room in the hotel and have sex, but Arpa disagreed.

But Arpa has assured me that she will tell me if her house is empty. I got more excited reading them and masturbated again. I left Arpa's phone in the previous place. Arpa came home in the evening.

I decided not to say anything this time. I'm curious to see the whole sex. Late at night, I resumed my spying. Orper's room is next to mine, so it is convenient for me. There was a balcony in front of the room for both of us.

I slowly opened the door of my room, came to the balcony, and peeked towards Arpa's window. I saw Arpa lying completely naked, with earphones in her ears.

And with one hand, the phone is raised to the face, and the other hand is fingering. Seeing this, my penis became salty. I came to my room and masturbated, thinking of my sister.

It's a pity to fuck your sister. I began to think of what to do! Later I thought, no, I will not fuck, but Shakib will enjoy it and see how it feels! Shakib also has a beautiful cousin! Naam Tazeen, whom Shakib also wants to fuck.

I could touch Shakib's cousin through Orpa, so I must sacrifice my sister. One morning, I saw where he was going, and he was in a hurry.

I asked my mother, "Where are you going?" Mother said my elder uncle's condition is severe, and he is going back there. It may be night, or he can stay at the hospital today.

Meanwhile, I saw that my father had gone to the office at 10:11 p.m. when he returned. Only me and I will stay at home. I then thought that the incident would happen today the incident would happen today if I left Arpa at home and went somewhere.

What you feel is what you do. After breakfast in the morning, I told Arpa that I was going out. Arpa just shook her head and said nothing.

I got ready, left the house, went inside the tea tong in front of the house, and sat in a corner so that I could not be seen from outside.

I sat there and waited for Shakib to come. After about fifteen to twenty minutes, Shakib came in a rickshaw. Three or four minutes after Shakib entered the building, I also entered the building, but instead of going to our apartment, I went up to the roof.

Coming out of the roof railing, I landed on the ceiling of the curtained window in front of Orper's room. An under-construction building was nearby, so there was no chance of falling. Now, I kept my eyes on the ventilator.

I see on the other side Arpa and Shakib are already half-naked and ready to kiss. Arpa wears only a bra and jeans pants, and Shakib wears a sando Genji and pants.

Shakib is holding and kissing Arpa very hard. It seems to tear the lips. Arpa is going low, and she is kissing.

After that, I saw that they loosened up a bit; now, Arpa unbuttoned Shakib's pants and put his hand inside the panty while Shakib was holding Arpa's breasts and kissing her.

Now Shakib lowered his face along the milk down Arpa's throat and started sucking the milk through the bra; Arpa was getting satisfaction. Arpa takes off her bra, Shakib starts sucking Arpa's milk nipple, and Arpa makes a satisfying noise.

Shakib made Arpa lie down on the bed and took off Arpa's pants, and inserted his finger in Arpa's cunt; Arpa shivered. Shakib keeps shaking Arpa with his fingers. Arpa was so excited she could no longer hold Shakib's head in her pussy.

Shakib is going to suck. Shakib sucked like this for a while, then Arpa released his semen. Now, Arpa pulled Shakib and kissed him, and Shakib laid down and opened his pants completely.

Shakib's eight-and-a-half-inch hard penis came out of the pants when he opened his pants.

Arpa said in surprise, "What happened!" Shakib, "Why didn't you like it?" Arpa, "That's enough!" That's why he started playing with Shakib's penny. Shakib then asked Arpa to take his penis in her mouth.

Arpa took it in her mouth and started sucking. My penis also stood up after watching my sister's fun. I masturbate from ceiling to ceiling. Then I went back to the ceiling and looked at the ventilator.

Arpa is still sucking Shakib's cock. Beachy sucks. Then Shakib poured jainaras into Arpa's mouth. Orpa swallowed the thick Yenras twice. Now Shakib put Orpa in a missionary position gently in Orpa's pussy.

Arpa shuddered. Shakib then started rubbing his penis against Arpa's pussy, making Arpa slowly reach the peak of excitement again. Now Shakib placed his penis in Arpa's tight pussy and pulled back his waist, and started fucking hard.

My younger sister Arpa cried. Shakib didn't understand, so Fuking started kissing Arpa. After kissing for two minutes, Shakib started fucking again.

Now the entire penis entered Orpa's vagina. Meanwhile, Arpa is petrified in pain. So Shakib began to kiss Arpa's neck and chest without hesitation.

This way, Arpa gradually became normal again and reached the peak of excitement. Now slowly, Shakib started to fuck. For the first few minutes, Orpa gritted her teeth but started humming with satisfaction when she was separated. Arpa, "ah ah ah ah ah ah ah uh…… louder…… ah ah ah ah ah… um…… 'm Shakib baby hard…… fuck harder ah ah hahaha… fuck harder baby fuck hard…… harder…" Shakib too.

Hearing the peak of excitement increased the pace of the fuck. Now, they change positions from missionary to cowboy style. Shakib is lying down. My younger sister Arpa set Shakib's cock in her pussy and jumped, "I'm coming, I'm coming…"

Arpa squirted water. As Shakib is experienced, he has not yet released his semen. He said to Orpa, "Where shall I pour my semen, honey?"

Arpa spread her legs and asked to let the cum out of her pussy. Shakib, without delay, set his penis in Orpa's pussy and continued to fuck hard. And after five minutes, they poured thick semen into Orpa's pussy.

Cum so thick and more that Orpa's pussy is overflowing. Now, both of them are tired and lie down. My money has stopped again. So I went up to the roof again and masturbated, looking at the ventilator; Shakib was taking my sister in doggy style.

Arpa can't make a sound even though her eyes are watering because of the pain. Shakib is covering Arpa's face with a cloth. After about 20 minutes of fucking, Shakib took the penis out of Orpa's pussy and poured his semen on Orpa's chest.

Then both of them lay down. After half an hour's rest, Shakib Orpak left the house with two more kisses. I came home half an hour later and found Arpa sleeping.

I didn't tell him anything. Since then, Arpa has often had sex with Shakib and has improved her figure a lot.

Then, once Shakib Arpa broke up, my younger sister Arpa was not crazy about less sex. He also had sex with our driver. I will tell that story another day.

But before Arpa Shakib's breakup, I also secretly fucked Shakib's cousin Tajin. That incident will be told another day.

My Baby in The Womb of My Brother's Wife

My baby in Brother's Wife's stomach, the sweet smell of Brother's Wife's cunt makes my mind go crazy, how I made Brother's Wife secretly pregnant.
I will tell you his story.

My name is Shubhra. I am passing high school now. I am 18 years old. My complexion is plump and fair. My penis size is 9 inches.

Come to the original story.

My brother's Wife's house is almost near Mine, just a few hands away. One day, I was passing by the road and saw my brother bathing in the pond. From that day, I decided not to kiss my brother's Wife even for a single day.

The incident happened that day. One day, there was no one at home, and suddenly, I saw my brother's Wife coming to my house.

That day, my Brother's Wife was not feeling well. My brother's Wife came and showed me a piece of paper. At first, I couldn't understand anything, but my brother's Wife suddenly started crying.

I said Brother Wife, what happened? Why are you crying? Brother Wife said your Dada will never be a father, I heard and understood what Brother Wife was trying to say.

In the meantime, Brother's Wife said I want your help, hearing this my mind started going crazy; I told Brother's Wife how can I help you, Brother Wife said I would spend the night with you; you will fuck me as you want, after hearing this, my chest was cut. Water without so many clouds,

Then, before I could say anything, Brother Wife threw me on the bed, after which Brother Wife lay on top of me.

By now, my penis is hard. I then told my Brother's Wife not to like this. I will kiss you in a different style.

Then I went up and brought two ropes and tied Brother Wife's hand to the bed, then started kissing Brother Wife only, then removed Brother Wife's saree and blouse completely; now Brother Wife is just a panty.

She is lying down in the bra with her hands crossed; after that, I put a handful of vermilion on the Brother Wife's forehead; by now, the Brother Wife is excited and twitching, and then I opened the Brother Wife's bra.

I began to dry my Wife's panties and started looking at her.

After that, I spread my Wife's legs and started to see the leakage of my Wife's pussy. Then I raised the waist with a pillow under my sister's waist so that I and my sister-in-law could have a comfortable table.

Then I opened my sister-in-law's bed and saw my sister-in-law's pussy. I saw her sister's two red cocks coming out.

Get up from me. When I got up, Brother's Wife lifted her legs with both hands.

All your semen will enter my stomach, and the baby will be born.

Then, two weeks passed at Brother Wife's house. One day, I heard a lot of noise, which indicated that Brother Wife's stomach was full. On the day of Romance, I went to Brother Wife's house.

Alienation and Physical Needs of Housewife's

Today, I present to you an incident that happened in my family. Before writing about the incident, I thought about whether to write it several times, but then I decided to write it as it is a story about a housewife, and she is none other than my mother.

My name is Jonny Pramanik. I am 22 years old, and I am home in Kolkata. My mother is a housewife, present age 44 years. Mother is beautiful 5" 4" in height, and very fair.

With age, Mom has become a bit fat and has a little belly fat, but she still looks beautiful and has a lot of hair on her body and both armpits. I often see mom's armpit hair when she wears a hand-cut maxi or blouse.

Mother used to save her body hair earlier, but in the last two or three years, she did not save anymore because her mental peace seemed lost.

I am the only child of my parents. My father works in Singapore, so once he goes abroad, he does not return for less than 4-6 months. Even though we are well-off, our father has always been rigorous and irritable.

At the end of the day, if there is lime from a little drink, I will be angry; even being cheeky does not reduce my mother and me. In the months he stays at home, not a day goes by that neither my mother nor I hear him yelling at me for some reason.

So, to tell the truth, we are better as mothers and sons when the father is abroad. May 14th was my mother's birthday, my father stayed at home 6 months before, then decided to take the COVID-19 vaccine and leave for Singapore on May 14th, so my mother was very disappointed that at least my father could have gone with Mother on her birthday.

But the father says, "If you stay at home, your income will not increase like this." So mother got very bored and packed father's luggage.

I feel awful for Mom, too. Finally, Dad left for the airport around 11 o'clock on May 14th.

We have rented a house next to my house to run a factory. He has two machines running there, and a boy is working there; his name is Saiful Alam Rabbi, Muslim by caste, age 24 years.

A little type black and chubby-cheeked. I have been very friendly with him since the beginning. He has been working in this factory for the past 3 years. His home is Murshidabad, so he returns home after two to three months away from Calcutta. I am called younger brother, and my mother is called aunt.

He does a lot of work for us, such as shopping for small items in the market and bringing flowers and sweets for Mother's puja every morning. In this way, he became like a member of our family; he used to talk a lot with his mother and sit on the stairs with the bag of goods in the machine.

At first, Saiful used to say he missed his mother very much, but then my mother told him, I am also your mother." Saiful has loved talking to his mother very much.

Mother feeds Saiful fish, meat, etc., every day at my house, calls him, and tells him that today Mother is taking her cooking. During those days, he saved on food expenses.

When the father was at home, his mother would secretly give him a bowl of meat or fish, and he would eat sitting in the factory. If the father were abroad, he would eat upstairs in our house.

Now, let's come to the main point. After Father left for the airport, I decided that I would buy cake for Mother and give Mother a surprise in the evening; tell Saiful so Saiful also said I would close the factory in the evening and go with me to buy cake because Saiful also knows my father by heart.

That evening, we both go together to buy a cake for Mom, and Saiful buys an imitation necklace for 250 rupees to gift to Mom.

When we returned home, Mother was not very happy to see all this, but she did not let us down; Mother cut the cake and fed it to us, and we fed it to Mother.

Then, the mother cooks Goat meat in the kitchen, and Saiful helps the mother talk hand in hand in the kitchen. As a result, the mother's indifference is removed a lot.

Then, at around 10:30, after our dinner, Saiful asked Mother, "Well, Aunty, can I stay with you today? Then I could talk with you till night; it is boiling in the factory. I will sleep in Jonny Bhai's room."

Mother looks at my face and wants to know what I like. I also say well, stay in my room and sleep. So, Mom made a mattress for her in my bedroom.

Then I sat till half past eleven and watched TV in my room. Mom and Saiful were sitting in the room chatting; Saiful talked a lot about their Murshidabad, and Mom laughed a lot listening to his funny jokes.

Then I asked them, "When are you going to sleep?"

Saiful says, "Not now, brother, one more hour. I will talk with Aunty then.

"The mother felt a little sleepy then but couldn't stop talking to him like this. So I went and lay down in my room. I was tired and fell asleep in no time. However, I woke up at 12:35 pm. I looked up from the bed and saw that Saiful was still not in the bed.

So I came out of my room but noticed the light was off. The ample light was coming from my mother's room window on the balcony, but the room door was closed. So I went to the window, closed the window and the AC was on, but the curtains were not drawn in my mother's room, and I could never have imagined what I had seen before.

Saiful is lying on the bed, holding his mother completely naked. Mother is only wearing a long panty. Saiful is squeezing the mother's milk and is constantly sucking and spitting in his mouth and biting the mother's neck and throat,

and licking the whole body. But the mother says occasionally, "Saiful, these things are not going well. My son will be troubled if he finds out."

You are Muslim. Our religion is different. Saiful is not taking anything, but he is hot with so much lust. Earlier, Saiful had fucked one of his cousins several times when he was 19 years old.

He told me because I used to talk to him about everything. His sister's family broke up with her husband, so Saiful used to give pleasure to his cousin.

Saiful used that experience in bed with his mother. He held his mother's hands and raised them above his head and saw that he was licking her hairy armpits.

I stand behind these windows and observe. A strange feeling of longing was coming into my mind. I felt like Saiful was thrown away, but seeing my mother's naked body again, my heart stopped.

I refuse to transcribe this content.

crossed my legs, and masturbated, imagining my mother for the first time in my life. I have masturbated a lot before, but I never imagined it, but this time, I did it. Then again, I went to the mother's window and saw Saiful lying down, hugging and kissing different parts of her body.

I sat on a small chair and hid by the window again around three o'clock in the morning. Saiful once again fucked my mother, lying on top of her, putting her finger in her pussy, and her mother was screaming a little in her throat.

In this way, both of them spent the whole night in bed without sleeping; it seemed as if Saiful and Mother both had the taste of birth today. As soon as I saw my mother sitting up, I immediately put the chair in its place and went to my room.

After some time, I realized Saiful had come and slept in my room. The following day, I woke up and saw that my mother had gone in early to take a bath and had removed the bed sheet in her room.

That day Saiful ejaculated inside their mother's vagina, it seemed that her mother took the pill, but since then, they used condoms every time they had intercourse which I often found lying in the drain of the septic chamber at the back of the house.

Maybe I went to the bank, or I went to borrow a book from a friend, or I went to hang out in a club; without two or four days, I see Nirod lying down, which then comes and goes in the enormous drain that comes out of the bathroom pipeline.

It happened last June. One Sunday, it was raining with low pressure all day. I went to the club to hang out and play a bit, but because of the rain, it wasn't possible to play, so I went back at twelve o'clock.

I came and knocked on the door several times, and my mother didn't open it, so I went around the back of the house. I unlocked the door and entered with a duplicate key attached to my bicycle key.

As soon as I entered the house, I realized that Saiful was fucking Mother inside the bathroom, and she was screaming at us, etc. I was forced to go to the club by bicycle through the house's back door.

At one o'clock in the afternoon, 20 minutes later, my mother called me to ask why I did not return home. I went home, saying I was hanging out; Mom didn't even realize I was back at 12 when she was busy making out in the bathroom.

I still haven't let them understand that I know everything, but I don't know how long it will last. And the mother is pleased now that Saiful is in her life and is fulfilling all the physical needs of the mother and also getting a lot of satisfaction in her pussy.

Their estrangement will continue like this, often without a day or two, until the father returns in October. Saiful sleeps with their mother two or three days a week in her room during heavy nights. A small door in the factory can be opened to enter my house.

I often watch them having sex at night whenever I want, sometimes in the doggy style; Mother takes a ride on Saiful's Penis. However, most of the mothers are sleeping on the bed.

Maybe I am masturbating a lot after seeing these things, but my main point is that homemakers who are involved in extraterrestrials are not bad in the first place; there is a lot of fault in this case also the heads of the house who are only busy making money but what does his wife expect from him. Don't worry about it.

My mother was perfect from the beginning, and I never noticed any bad behavior from my mother since childhood or before; this is the first time in my life that my mother got involved in an extramarital affair, even in her 40s with a boy of her age.

How much suffering and pain will people endure and spend their lives indifferent and lonely? Thinking of these seven and five, I pretend not to know everything. Maybe when my father returns home, all this will stop.

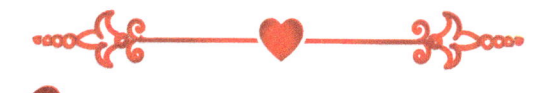

My Baby in The Belly of Elder Brother's Wife

The elder brother's wife looks like a brunette and a small elephant. Her breasts are big and drooping. She has a big belly, and her ass moves when she walks.

I used to talk freely with him about everything. We used to have sexual talks, too. She is very similar to my wife, so whatever I do with my wife, my wife used to tell her everything. Brother owns a shop, so they rent a house in the city.

One day I went to his house to give him the invitation card. I rang the bell, and after some time, my Elder brother's wife came and opened the door. He was happy to see me and asked me to go inside.

I went inside, and he asked me to sit. I sat on the sofa in his room. He sat me down and brought breakfast. Both are sitting on the sofa, eating breakfast and talking. I asked where the brother and the child were.

The elder brother's wife said their brother was in the shop, and the kid was in school. My elder brother's wife asked about my wife, and I said.

The elder brother's wife also asked when we would take the baby. I said it's time to have fun, so I'll take the kid in a few days. Elder brother's wife said, are you kidding? I said it must be fun.

I talk to my wife about everything, so I don't say anything. The elder brother's wife says to have fun but to take the baby on time. I said, "Hmm, I will take it when it's time."

The elder brother's wife said I also want to have another child. Why did I take the delay? My elder brother's wife said I tried, but it's not working. I said Brother, cannot at night? The elder brother's wife said it could, but it is not happening. I said with a smile if you want, I can try.

Elder brother's wife also said with a smile that your brother also does well said I could do better. Elder brother's wife said I know you don't want to come down when you go up.

Sister has a lot of fun. I said if you want, I will give it to you too. The elder brother's wife said it would be better if you had fun. Everyone wants to have fun.

I said then why away? Come and have fun.

Elder brother's wife said doesn't do the damn fun. Go and get a wife. I said there was no need to go home. It's three days today. Elder brother's wife said, oh, what's your problem? I said, "Hmm, a lot of trouble." Elder brother's wife said then you have to give and take fun. Why are you late?

As soon as the wife said that, I went to the wife and started kissing her lips and pressing milk. By this time, Elder brother's wife was starting to move over my tight-hole pants. The elder brother's wife was wearing a maxi but nothing underneath.

I asked if the bride was ready for me to come. My elder brother's wife said I can't stand the heat, so I stay open when no one is home. I lifted my wife's maxi and put my hand on her pussy.

His pussy was lightly hairy and completely wet with juice. I said to my wife, so much sexual juice came out of words? The elder brother's wife said there is juice in your words, so why don't you leave? Did I say so or not? The elder brother's wife said it today and before talking to you.

I have to go to the bathroom to wash. I said earlier I would have been joking. Elder brother's wife said I didn't give it before, give it today. I said today, I will make fun of you, honey. Elder brother's wife said today. I want to have fun, know.

Then I went to bed with my Elder brother's wife. I took it to my wife's bed and laid her down. I saw her pussy blacker than her body. I asked the wife if it was black. Not only does the brother give it, but there is someone else.

The wife said after marriage, your grandfather gave it. And today, you, I said before marriage? The wife said that when the vagina is there, the burning of the vagina will be there. I said how many people are cleaning your web.

The elder brother's wife said that many people took chances, but one person managed to fuck. I fucked my wife's legs and put my penis in her pussy. Then the wife entered the juicy pussy with light pressure.

I started fucking slowly. The elder brother's wife is so fat that she can't fuck from below. Just fucking while lying down. The stomach is also moving with milk. I am looking at Elder's brother's wife's face with both hands and kissing her. After about fifteen minutes of fucking, both of us are completely sweaty and alone.

Sweat drips from my forehead, and my wife laughs. The elder brother's wife is laughing. I spit from my mouth, and she took that, too. After some more sex, I told my wife that I would be done. The elder brother's wife said to put it inside. Did I say really?

The elder brother's wife said your brother also gave it inside, but it is not working. Can you let me see if it works today? I said that I would love to be the mother of my child. Elder brother's wife said your brother has one, or the other is yours.

I said ok and increased the speed of the fuck. After some time of fucking, hot semen is going in the pussy of the wife. The elder brother's wife has her eyes closed. He says with his eyes closed, don't take it out.

I said why? The elder brother's wife said to let the whole tie in. I put the penis inside the vagina for about 5 minutes. Then I went to the bathroom and got clean. I came and saw Elder's brother's wife lying like that with her eyes closed. I asked if it would happen once more or not.

If the Elder brother's wife said, it would be good. I got dressed, and my Elder brother's wife came fresh. We talked for some time, and my brother came. I left after having lunch with my brother. A few days later, my wife told me there was happy news.

I said what news? The wife said the baby was in the belly of the mother-in-law. I have been trying for a long time now. I must eat sweets one day. The wife said, "Hmm, I will go one day." The finger didn't give, and then Brother Wife blinked at me.

I continued to poke the pussy with my finger in Brother Wife's vagina, and Brother Wife got excited and uttered the sound of "Uh, ah" from her mouth. I brought it to my nose and smelled it was a few grains of goo, then kissed Brother Wife's pussy and inserted my tongue in Brother Wife's pussy and got excited by smelling Brother Wife's pussy.

Then I put my hand on the hair of Brother Wife's pussy and then lick the pussy with my mouth.

Then I took off my pant and put my penis in my Brother's Wife's pussy, and my Brother's Wife screamed and said leave me, son of a whore, then I put my penis in my Brother's Wife's pussy like this, and kept on fucking, and in this way, for 30 minutes I made Brother Wife's pussy ultimately cave. Then came the perfect time: after the semen came out, Brother's Wife understood and said, "Open my hand." The next day, the Elder brother's wife called and said I could become a mother again, thanks to you. I also said thank you for making me a father.

Mona's Taste of Motherhood

Hello guys, I'm Markus. Today, I will share an incident from my life. The incident was in 2018. I left the village to study and left the hostel after studying in the city.

I did not rent a house, a small house with two rooms. I couldn't cook and manage the house. So, with the help of the house janitor, I fixed a Home Worker. Her name is Mona. That is the heroine of this story.

Let mc give some details of Mona for the reader's friends. He was 25 or 26 years old, had a dark complexion, and was slightly fat. Her breasts will be 34, but 36, overall 34-28-34 figure

Mona is a little reserved. He used to talk to me about many things. He worked and worked well with his words, so I didn't mind him talking too much.

I loved listening to him. At that time, I was freelancing, finishing most of the work at night and between ten in the morning. I used to listen to him when I didn't have work in the morning. Thus, we develop relationships.

I learned from them that she had been married for six years and had no children and that her husband used to accuse her of barrenness and sometimes even beat her. She used to call her husband old and make various jokes. Where did he get the impression of her husband's disability?

He was honest and detailed while talking too much. So I give him a house key to do housework in my absence or sleep.

However, a couple of months passed like this. But one day, I saw how he became silent, just working with a sad face. I asked the reason a couple of times, and he avoided it.

Three days, he was passed like this. On the third day, he finished work and came to say goodbye; that day, the sky was covered with dark clouds, and a storm was coming. So I asked him to come out after a while, and he agreed. We both went to my bedroom.

I stood in front of him and asked the reason for his silence. This is the first time he opened his mouth about it. She said her husband came intoxicated and beat her in front of a slum dweller, calling her a childless woman (infertile).

Saying this, he suddenly hugged me and started crying. Her warm tears soaked my Dress. I was a bit surprised. After a while, I started feeling the touch of her round and soft milk on my chest; her hard nipples were poking me, and I was feeling horny. Then suddenly, I kissed her on the cheek, and my heartbeat multiplied at the thought. However, she stops crying and kisses me on the face [somewhere between the cheek and lips]. Then we looked into each other's eyes.

The two were so close, the rain-bathed weather upon him. Due to these reasons, my Penis got hard and started touching Mona's stomach. Mona understood my situation and smiled, and that smile hypnotized me.

I pushed her down on the bed and started taking off my clothes. He was half lying on the bed, looking at me. When I pulled out my 7-inch hard cock, she looked at it with a crazy look. I jumped and unbuttoned her blouse. Her milky nipples peeked out as she unbuttoned the two buttons. Immediately, I opened the whole blouse and exposed her breasts.

Round white milk on the upright brown, what a beauty! I pressed her milk for some time, took it in my mouth and sucked it. The saltiness of the sweat-soaked milk increased my thirst. He is taking a deep breath.

After some time, I took off her saree petticoat and stripped her naked. I saw her curly thick hairy pussy. Both are naked; outside, the sun plays with the clouds.

I started caressing her, and she kept responding, no words on anyone's lips, only breathing and ahh ahh sounds. I could not hold myself back.

Taking his opinion on the gesture, I made him cry and prepared to fuck. As soon as the 3-inch thick cock was pushed into the juicy pussy, Mona gasped and moaned and raised her hands to see a hairy armpit.

However, I started fucking hard, it was raining heavily outside. His screams are heard over the sound of the rain; ah ah ah mother ah ah maa, Random scream. After ten minutes, I lied down and put Mona on the floor, and started fucking from below.

His 34-size tits are jumping with enthusiasm as he fucks, and his face is dripping with saliva. After 5 minutes of fucking like this, his semen came out, my thighs were wet with hot semen. He leaned over and kissed me, and our saliva became one. After two minutes of foreplay, fuck again in the missionary position for about 20 minutes. Thus, my time draws near.

Penis was going to take it out of the vagina, but in extreme excitement, Mona twisted it and grabbed me. I also continued to fuck hard for 3-4 hours in excitement and then ejaculated in the back of the vagina.

Mona's pussy was filled with a cup of hot semen. He pulled her towards him and began kissing her nose, lips, and cheeks, wild kisses. Hugging her tightly on her chest, the soft bosom kisses lay on my chest. Her a.a.a orgasm was still going on. After some time, I lay down next to him.

I saw the injury mark on his shoulder and clapped my hands. "Stay!" he said. Then he said, "Let me clean you up". Mona took me to the bathroom. I sat on the commode. She started washing my Penis with utmost care. The week was getting excited by his soft touch.

He tells Penis, "A lot of fun," and kisses him softly as he washes Penis, by which time he stands with his head held high. Mona slowly moved up and down, current running through my body.

Then took it in the mouth and started sucking, showing me paradise. No sensation with eyes closed. The mouth kept coming out quietly. After 2-3 minutes of his magic sucking, I leave the material in his mouth, but the quantity is small.

He swallows it whole. Thus ends our Play Fuking. He gets up and gets dressed. I stay on. At the farewell, he asked me:

Mona: Will you be the father of my child?

Me: (Shocked) [What does this whore say!]

Mona: (Laughs) Remember, I am a childless woman

Me: I didn't believe it

Mona: (patting her hand on cheek) No matter what happens, your name will not come; you gave me so much happiness!!!

Give her Child in the name of the elder (husband). Don't worry

He takes the exit. I watched with mixed feelings.

However, from the next day, my relationship took a turn; hugs & kisses became a regular affair.

I used to avoid kissing on the lips; thousands of slum girls brushed their teeth with ash coal, and it smelled terrible. But kissing on the lips was his fantasy. I don't necessarily agree.

Days were going well; I stood in the kitchen and played with her milk; she sucked my money and showed me paradise, sometimes I also gave pleasure by eating hairy pussy, and two or three days a week, I used to have sex; there was a stock of condoms in the house.

A few weeks later, one morning, I heard the sound of the lock being opened in my sleep. When I opened my eyes, it wasn't half past nine. Mona was so early!.

I didn't have the strength to look up, I stayed on the bed. Suddenly, I felt a kiss on my lips. I smelled it, it was Mona. Without opening my eyes, I pulled him to sleep on my back.

After kissing him deeply, he rolled over and slept next to me. I said:

Me: So much love! What a matter!

Mona: You Father, I'm not a slave, I'm not a whore. Even though I broke down with anxiety inside, I smiled with joy outside, comforting him. He says:

Mona: Make eye pies. Huda doesn't like happy news.

Me: Do what you like.

Mona: My liver

He goes and makes pies, blows hot pies, feeds me, kisses my lips, and eats from my mouth. Lose yourself in joy, which pleases. As the months went by happily, her big belly became visible. After seven months, he took leave, saying:

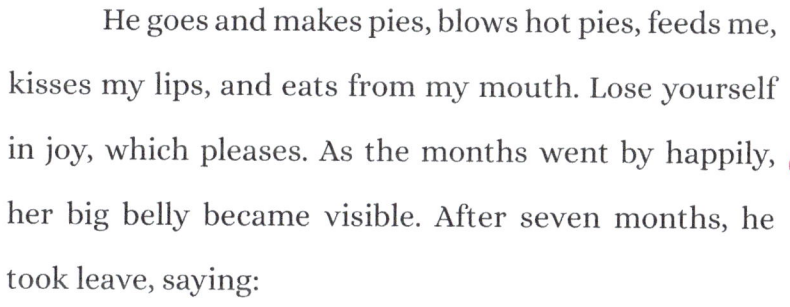

Mona: I couldn't come anymore.

Me: No problem, you need rest

Mona: My mother-in-law is really into work. Lisa.

Me: Ok.

Mona: See Tare again something…

Me: None of that will happen… I am only yours. Hearing this, he smiles proudly, hugs me from the right side (for the big belly), pulls my head, kisses me deeply, and then leaves.

The next day, Lisa (Mona's niece) comes to work. She is an 18-year-old girl with a dark complexion, a thin body, and almost no milk (small). Lisa is short-spoken. When I asked about Mona, she answered in a few words and focused on work. How many months have passed like this?

On March 18 (2019), Lisa came by herself and told Mona she had a son who looked like Mona. I was slightly startled if I looked like I would be finished! Let's live this trip! I was also thrilled. After another fifteen days, he passed. Suddenly, the clock struck 11 o'clock, and Lisa was not seen; I thought she might not come a day, so I ordered breakfast.

Around 11:30, a bell rang; I opened the door and saw Mona, *our* son, in her arms. Took him in quickly. He gave the boy in my lap and said, "Look, this is your father." He said, "Child nose is like yours". Then she sat naked and breastfed the boy. I sat next to her and watched. When the boy falls asleep, he says, "It's the Child's Father's turn."

I am also breastfed in any lap; eating feels good. Later, he says, "The old man does not live happily; this is his son, and your son has strength! Cow is one. He is naming Child Yashin." I said wow, good name. The next day, he left it with his son's sister. Everything becomes normal between us. The extra is her breast milk. Her milk supply was good, and she was feeding often. Once breast milk tea is fed, it feels great to eat, slightly sweeter than cow's milk...

A few more months pass like this. In my early 20s, I had to move to another area for work and leave home, and that's how our relationship ended. But still, sometimes I can't find my son on the phone. I kept a number of Mona. I'm happy to hear that Mona's husband takes good care of his son.

This was the untold truth of my life. Here. I was fortunate that I didn't get trapped or get sexually transmitted diseases after making a maid a mother. That may not be the case for everyone. So it is better not to do these things without a condom in the excitement.

Conclusion

*A*s you turn the final page of "The Romantic Boy Short Erotical Story Book," we hope your heart is filled with the warmth and passion that only true romance can bring. Fiona Rose has meticulously crafted these stories to capture the essence of love in its most compelling forms, providing an unforgettable experience for romance lovers anywhere.

You've journeyed through tales of intense desire, tender moments, and captivating encounters, each designed to pull you deeper into a world where love reigns supreme. Imagine reliving these moments repeatedly, savoring each detail, and feeling the rush of emotions with every read. Whether you devoured this book in one sitting or savored each story over time, the impact of these heartfelt narratives is undeniable.

Now, envision sharing this experience with others. Gift this book to friends who crave the thrill of romance, or revisit these stories whenever you need a reminder of love's enchanting power. Fiona Rose's engaging storytelling entertains and inspires, leaving you with a sense of longing and a desire for more.

Don't let the journey end here. Explore other works by Fiona Rose and immerse yourself in erotic romance. Follow her on social media, join her mailing list, and stay updated on new releases and exclusive content. Your next adventure in love and passion awaits.

Thank you for choosing "The Romantic Boy Short Erotical Story Book." We hope it has brought joy, excitement, and a touch of magic to your reading experience. Purchase additional copies, leave a review, and share your thoughts to help spread the love. Remember, romance is a journey best enjoyed together.

Thank you

Made in the USA
Coppell, TX
11 February 2025